Qubit's Incubator

by

Charley Brindley

charleybrindley@yahoo.com

www.charleybrindley.com

Edited by

Karen Boston

Website https://bit.ly/2rJDq3f

Cover art by

Charley Brindley
© 2020

i

Printed in the United States of America

First Edition April 2020

This book is dedicated to
the memory of

James Seth Brindley

Some of Charley Brindley's books
have been translated into:
Italian
Spanish
Portuguese
French
Dutch
Chinese
and
Russian

iii

Other books by Charley Brindley

1. *Oxana's Pit*
2. *The Last Mission of the Seventh Cavalry*
3. *Raji Book One: Octavia Pompeii*
4. *Raji Book Two: The Academy*
5. *Raji Book Three: Dire Kawa*
6. *Raji Book Four: The House of the West Wind*
7. *Hannibal's Elephant Girl*
8. *Cian*
9. *Ariion XXIII*
10. *The Last Seat on the Hindenburg*
11. *Dragonfly vs Monarch: Book One*
12. *Dragonfly vs Monarch: Book One*
13. *The Sea of Tranquility 2.0 Book One: Exploration*
14. *The Sea of Tranquility 2.0 Book Two: Invasion*
15. *The Sea of Tranquility 2.0 Book Three*
16. *The Sea of Tranquility 2.0 Book Four*
17. *Sea of Sorrows, Book Two of The Rod of God*
18. *Do Not Resuscitate*
19. *Hannibal's Elephant Girl, Book Two*
20. *The Rod of God, Book One*
21. *Henry IX*

Coming Soon

22. *Dragonfly vs Monarch: Book Three*
23. *The Journey to Valdacia*
24. *Still Waters Run Deep*
25. *Ms Machiavelli*
26. *Ariion XXIX*
27. *The Last Mission of the Seventh Cavalry Book 2*
28. *Hannibal's Elephant Girl, Book Three*

See the end of this book for details about the others

iv

Contents

Chapter One

West Chelsea, New York City

Tuesday morning, 10 a.m.

"Thank you for the opportunity."

Catalina took the offered straight-back oak chair. She watched the man behind the desk as he read her CV.

Thirtyish, confident, well-dressed. I wonder if he's the owner or manager?

She adjusted her short blue skirt, then rested her tightly clasped hands on the iPad in her lap.

Victor Templeton was clean-shaven, with a little gray sprinkled throughout his sun-bitten hair. His face looked weathered, tired. He watched Catalina for a moment, but her steady gaze didn't waver. He wrote the number "7" on his notepad.

"Whatcha got..." he glanced at her CV, "Miss Catalina Saylor?"

Catalina's hand shot to the right side of her thigh,

where she patted her skirt.

They're gone! She panicked. *How could I lose them?*

Her heart raced. Jerking her hand one way then another, she finally felt a familiar object, then the second one.

There you are. Thank God!

The concealed pocket held her treasures. All her skirts and dresses had pockets hidden within the folds of cloth. She never wore pants or shorts. Without her talisman, she would be lost.

"Sound imaging for the blind," she said in answer to his question.

Victor spun a yellow pencil on his desk. "Hmm...like a bat's echolocation?"

Catalina's breathing returned to normal as her heart rate slowed. "Something like that, but using AI to convert the radar bounces into a non-visual image."

Victor scribbled the number "8" on his notepad. "Non-visual image." It wasn't a question; he repeated her phrase as if trying to give it substance. "Being fed into the blind person's optic nerve?"

"No. To her fingertips, making her surroundings into a tactile image."

"You have ten minutes to sell this idea to me."

Catalina tossed her head to the side, like a girl with a long strand of hair irritating her face; however, her short chocolate-brown hair, neatly brushed and pushed back, hardly covered her ears. A little blush on her cheeks would have added depth to her statuesque beauty, but she never wore makeup, thinking it was a waste of time. Maybe someday, if she ever wanted to advertise her availability for dating.

She opened her iPad and placed it on the desk,

facing him. Reaching over the top, she pressed a key.

A stick-figure with a long cane materialized on the stark white screen.

Catalina sat back, keeping her eyes on Victor.

As he watched the iPad, the figure mobilized and made its way along a sketched-in street. The figure slowly morphed into a human form—a woman, then clothing was added; a flowery blouse and long skirt, both in black and white.

She tapped her cane on the sidewalk, feeling her way along.

The sidewalk and buildings took on more detail as the sounds of murmured voices and traffic came from the iPad speakers.

Color was added to the woman's clothing as she made her way through the passing pedestrians; chartreuse for the skirt, and a shocking orange for her blouse. The outlined buildings became shops, with books and jewelry displayed in the windows, while a convenience store came into view ahead of her.

"Who did this animation?"Victor asked.

"I did," Catalina said. "Most of it."

He used his pen to slash through the "8" and wrote "9" beside it.

The blind woman came to a street crossing and stopped when the end of her cane dropped off the edge of the curb.

She tilted her head, listening.

"Anyone there?" Her voice came from the speakers.

A girl, maybe ten years old, came to her side. "What's wrong?"

"I'm blind. Can you help me across the street? This is Forty-seventh, right?"

"Yes, it is." The girl took her hand. "What happened to your eyes?"

"Afghanistan."

"Step down." The girl led the woman off the curb and into the street. "We can cross now. You were hurt in the war?"

"Yes. What's your name?"

"Monica. We're in the middle of the street, but we still have the light."

"Do you live nearby?"

"Two blocks. Mama sent me to the store for baking powder. Get ready to step up on the curb."

The white cane tapped ahead of the woman. When it touched the curb, she felt for the height.

"If you can't see, why do you wear sunglasses?"

After stepping up on the sidewalk, the woman felt for her glasses and removed them.

"Oh," Monica said.

The woman's eyes were cloudy orbs, scared and misshapen.

"I see what happened. I'm sorry."

"Don't be. Thanks for helping me."

"What's your name?" the girl asked.

"I'm Cindy."

A knock came at the office door, then a young woman with red hair peeked in. "Your next appointment is here."

Victor kept his eyes on the video as he held up his hand toward her in a 'Tell the applicant to wait a few minutes' gesture.

Catalina stared at the redhead. *Dangly earrings. Perfectly shaped, gold enclosing jade stones. Ovals!*

The young woman glanced at Catalina, then nodded to Victor and closed the door.

The video suddenly rewound back to the stick figure in the first frame. It started as before, but now, as the animation progressed, the white cane was equipped with a shiny metal cylinder wrapping around the shaft, near the handgrip. A bracelet of similar design circled the woman's left wrist. Both had blinking green LEDs while emitting a soft beeping sound.

When the woman came to the curb, she shifted the cane to her right hand, then held up her left, with the palm forward. The beeping sound accelerated. She cocked her head to the side, then after a moment she slowly shifted her open palm to her left. She paused there, then moved her hand all the way around to the right.

The blind woman waited until the sounds of traffic stopped, then held out her palm to her left, apparently checking for any cars turning right, and into her path.

Satisfied it was clear, she stepped off the curb and walked confidently forward, avoiding a yellow taxi that had stopped halfway into the crosswalk.

She was soon on the other side of the street and striding toward her destination.

Victor leaned back in his chair as Catalina took her iPad, turned it toward her, and clicked off the video.

"Nice. I understand the concept," he said. "But not only will it require some very dense coding, you'll have to work out the computer-human interface."

"I know it won't be easy."

"Are you a coder?"

"I did most of the programming of the demo video."

"Where did you learn to code?"

"I'm teaching myself."

Victor marked out the "9" and wrote "10." "Why

do you need Qubit's Incubator?"

"For a place to work. And I'll need electronic test equipment, too."

"Why can't you work at home?"

"I share a small apartment with a roomie who loves to party and make lots of noise."

"You don't party and make noise?"

"I used to."

"How old are you?"

"Twenty-two."

"No other place to live?"

"I can't afford a place by myself, or the equipment I need."

"Your parents?"

"Not an option."

"Do you have a job?"

She nodded.

"How much do you make?"

Catalina hesitated, wrinkling her brow as she gazed at a picture on the wall behind Victor. It was a large horizontal oval containing Egyptian hieroglyphs. The symbols were embossed characters chiseled into stone.

"I work in a café." *Die with...*She tried to work out the translation. "With extra shifts and tips, I clear around four thousand a month." *Die with what?*

"And you can't get your own place on that?"

"I have...um...other expenses." *Die with memories...but what is that last part?*

He marked out the "10" and went back to "8." "What are they?"

"Why do you need to know all this?"

"Miss Saylor, do you want help from the Incubator?"

"Of course I do."*Dreams!*

"Then I need enough information to make a decision. If you're over your head in credit card debt and all you can do is make minimum payments, you'll never get out from under that load of debt working at a café."

Die with memories, not dreams. She smiled. *All within a perfect oval frame.*

She took a deep breath, examined her nails for a moment, then exhaled. "I dated a guy for almost a year. I thought we had a future together, but he tricked me into running my four credit cards up to the limit, then when we couldn't charge anything more, he bailed on me."

Victor lined through the "8" and wrote "10" again. "You see that door?" He pointed across the room, opposite from the door the young woman had opened earlier.

Her shoulders slumped. She nodded. "You're rejecting me?"

"Go through that door, pick out a vacant desk, and get organized. Then–"

Catalina squealed with delight, jumped from the chair, and stepped to the end of his desk. "I'm accepted?! I can't believe it. Can I hug you?"

"No. As I was saying, come back to see me at four this afternoon. Now, wipe that smile off your face and go find a desk. You've got thirty days to prove yourself."

"Yes, sir." She actually did wipe her hand across her broad smile, leaving behind a serious frown. "I'm on it." She hurried toward the door.

Victor smiled as he made a note on the edge of her application—30 days.

Chapter Two

Catalina pushed open the door to find a large warehouse. She stepped inside, letting the door close silently behind her.

The place had apparently been some sort of assembly factory many years ago.

The underside of the corrugated ceiling was about seventy feet above her head. Twenty feet up, a wide balcony ran along the sides of the building. Many doors lined the outside perimeter of the balcony. A few were open, but she couldn't see inside the rooms.

A large block-and-tackle hung from a steel girder. A metal hook, the size of a wrestler's arm, was suspended below the rusting block on a rusting chain. Someone had hung a large doll from the hook.

Catalina tilted her head and squinted at the doll, which had a noose around its neck.

Is that Donald Trump?

The central open area of the huge floor had thirty desks placed haphazardly about. Most were occupied by men and women concentrating on their computers or building models of strange devices.

One young man glanced up at her, then returned to assembling a tall Tinker Toy gadget on his desk.

Surrounding the open area was a collection of

cubicle work areas. She saw several rows of these cubicles, forming semicircles around and away from the open area, like an amphitheater. She could see into some of them, and most were occupied.

Find a vacant desk, he said.

Catalina walked through the open area, passing around a few cleared desks.

It's so quiet in here.

Someone coughed. A chair squeaked. No other sounds could be heard. But there was an air of intensity about the place, like a classroom during a calculus exam.

She came to an unoccupied cubicle. She placed her iPad on the cleared desk and tried the chair. Leaning back, she gazed about at the blank walls of the workspace.

Just needs a few pictures to...

"Hey, Pissant."

She almost fell over backwards. "W-what?" Looking up, she saw a young Black woman peeking over the wall.

"Pissants live in the bullpen," the woman said. "You don't become a drone until you've accomplished something."

"Drone?"

"This cubicle don't belong to you." The Black woman disappeared.

Did she call me a 'pissant?'

Catalina collected her iPad and went to the open area of the bullpen.

She found a desk with a Scotch tape dispenser, stapler, pencils, and an old-school computer.

Sitting at the desk, she opened her iPad and searched for a Wi-Fi connection.

"What're you doing?"

She jerked around to see a scruffy old man with

one hand on his hip and the other holding a steaming cup of coffee.

"I-I-I'm..."

"I-I-I'm..." he mocked her in a singsong voice. "Get out of my chair."

Catalina grabbed her iPad, stood, and backed away. "Sorry."

"Over there."

The old man pointed with his coffee cup toward the edge of the bullpen, where a gray metal desk and matching chair stood like salvaged government-issued office furniture relegated to the outliers.

She went to the desk, and when she sat in the chair, she could feel the cold metal through the fabric of her skirt.

The desk was turned away from the others in the bullpen, facing a brick wall that looked more like a weathered outside wall than the inside of a building.

Her hand, as if by its own accord, felt for the pocket in her skirt. Slipping her hand into the pocket, her fingers searched for something. When they touched the smooth surface of one of the objects, she smiled.

High above was a large skylight providing a view of the blue sky, but only a dim gray glow came through the ages of caked-on grime.

Opening her iPad, Catalina searched again for a Wi-Fi signal. Finally, she found 'Qubit Inc.' The curser blinked, then a message popped up, demanding, 'PASSWORD.'

She looked over her shoulder at the other pissants. *They're not going to be any help.*

The 'low battery' LED began to blink on her iPad.

She saw an electrical outlet embedded in the brick wall, twenty feet away. She took the charging cord from her purse.

Six feet long. How am I going to reach that outlet? Move the desk? Glancing at the others, she shook her head. *Invisible little pissant. That's all I am. Do I really want to do this? At least at home I can charge up my computer and get online.*

Turning back to her iPad, she tried 'qubit' for a password, then 'Victor,' but neither was acceptable.

If I try a third time, it might lock...

"Bullpen."

Catalina turned to see a man standing behind her. "What the hell? I took a cubicle, and someone told me to go to the bullpen. I went there and found a desk. Then some snippy guy told me to get out of his chair and come over here. So now I guess this is your desk and I have to go back to the middle of the floor and wait to see if any desk remains unused. Why is everyone so mean in this place?"

The man smiled, watching her smolder.

"Well, at least you can smile," she said, then closed her computer and rolled up the power cord.

He was about thirty-five, heavyset, with a shaved head and thick black beard. His faded blue shirt had long sleeves buttoned at the wrist.

He toyed with a red rubber band using a sleight-of-hand trick where the rubber band seemed to flip from one pair of fingers to the other two when he folded them into his palm, then opened them. Using his thumb so smoothly in his palm, it almost seemed like magic as the band jumped back and forth.

Tattoos of beautiful jaguars slipped from beneath his cuffs, sinking their bloody claws into the backs of his hands.

Catalina stood, ready to go look for another desk.

"'Bullpen' is the password." His voice was soft, unthreatening. He sipped from his bottle of Coke.

"Oh." She sat back down. "Thank you."

She opened her iPad and typed in the password.

'Qubit's Incubator. Connected, secured.'

After opening a browser, she went online to her webpage.

A blurred view of the Alps filled the screen. As the panoramic image sharpened, it slipped into a video from the viewpoint of a drone aircraft approaching the tallest mountain.

"The Matterhorn!" the guy whispered.

Catalina nodded as she watched the screen.

The drone turned slightly to the right, flying toward a huge glacier. As the video zoomed in closer, a red dot appeared on the snow-covered ice field. The dot grew larger and became a woman in a red jumpsuit. She waved to the drone. Closer still, and one could see skis, ski poles, and a yellow backpack.

When the drone was a few feet away, the woman smiled, adjusted her goggles in place, then pushed off.

The drone turned to follow her down the slope as if it were on a pair of skis fifteen feet behind her.

"Wow," the guy exclaimed. "You did the CGI?"

"Yeah. That twenty seconds of footage took three weeks of coding."

"I believe it. Beautiful."

"Thank you." She looked up at him. "I'm Catalina."

"Adu Dhabi Wilson."

"Really?"

"I was born in Abu Dhabi, in the United Arab Emirates, when my parents were stationed at the diplomatic mission there."

"So, I should call you 'Adu' or 'Will?'"

"Most people call me 'Joe' or 'Pissant.'"

She smiled. "I like 'Joe.'"

"It seems you need an extension cord."

"Yes," Catalina said.

"And desk supplies."

She nodded.

"Come on."

Joe led her thorough the bullpen, where half of the twenty-four people looked up from their work, glaring at him as if he were a turncoat.

She followed him along an aisle between cubicles.

Outside the last ring of workspaces, he motioned to his left. "Kitchenette." A few steps farther. "Bathrooms. And..." He came to a door beyond the bathrooms. "Supply room."

He pushed open the door to reveal rows of metal shelves.

"Cool," Catalina said. "Pencils, tape, staplers, tablets–"

"Extension cords." He handed her a new cord, along with a surge protector.

"Great. Can I take some other things?"

"Sure. Take whatever you want. All this stuff's for everyone's use."

She loaded her arms and started for her desk. "What's the deal with the bullpen and the cubicles?"

"Something to drink?" Joe asked as he headed for the kitchenette.

"Yes."

He tossed his empty Coke bottle in a trash bin and poured a cup of coffee. "If you take the last cup of coffee, start a new pot. We put away two or three gallons a day. Sodas and juice are in the fridge. If you see something running low, add it to this list." He waved toward a dry-erase board on the wall beside the fridge. 'Jif Crunchy Peanut Butter. Mayo. M&Ms' were listed on the board. "We take turns on runs to the grocery store." He opened a small canister. "This is petty cash for the store. The Good Fairy replenishes the cash when it runs low."

Opening the fridge, he showed her the contents— Coke, 7-Up, Mountain Dew, Dr. Pepper, juice...

"A bottle of OJ, please," she said.

He reached for the orange juice, glanced at her

load of supplies, then balanced it on top of her stack.

Closing the fridge, he led her back toward her desk. "When you're accepted to incubate, they toss you into the bullpen to sink or swim. If, after the first thirty days, you're still a viable tissue mass, you get a cubicle. Two months later, if the gods smile upon you, you rise to the top." He pointed up.

Above them, Catalina saw the balcony going around the four sides of the bullpen and cubicle area. Two circular staircases led up to it. To the right, where Joe pointed, were fifteen doors. Some of them were open, but most were closed.

"What are they?" she asked.

"Private offices."

"For who?"

"Monarchs."

"Wow. And those, too?" She nodded to fifteen more doors on the left balcony.

A young woman with a Dr. Pepper went up one of the staircases and turned to her right, while the redhead from the outside office climbed the opposite staircase and went to one of the offices. She didn't knock at the closed door, instead pushing it open and stepping inside.

"No. That side's the dorm."

"What?"

"Dorm rooms."

"Who gets those?"

"The lucky ones." Joe sighed. "How I would love to live up there." They watched the other woman go into one of the dorm rooms. "Come on," Joe said. "Let's get you settled. I've got six days to become a drone, or die."

"Will you make it?"

"Most pissants die of self-inflicted trauma before they metamorphosize into worker drones."

Catalina leaned close to Joe. "Who's that old pissant? The curmudgeon?"

"William Thomas Edison."

"What's he working on, a newfangled plow?"

Joe laughed. "He's designing a system to collect water from the air using nanotubes."

"Really? What's inside the nanotubes?"

"No one knows. He's not talking until he makes it work."

* * * * *

After Catalina ran the extension cord from the outlet to her desk, she plugged in her iPad to charge the battery.

On her way back to the supply room, she stopped by the restroom. While washing her hands, her eyes fell on the cap of the cold-water faucet.

After drying her hands on a paper towel, she took two objects from her skirt pocket. The first was a small oval brass nameplate with 'Evangeline Psychiatric Hospital' engraved into the metal. The second was a micro screwdriver. She sipped the nameplate back into her pocket and removed the leather sheath she'd fashioned for screwdriver.

Working the sharp edge under the chrome cap on the faucet, she popped it off.

She rinsed the metal cap and dried it.

Holding it to the light, she admired the curlicue 'C' imprinted in the cap.

"Sweet," she whispered. "A perfect oval."

After removing the hot water cap, with its pretty 'H', Catalina cleaned it and dropped both caps into her pocket. She then slipped the screwdriver into its sheath and put it away.

In the storeroom, she found a desk lamp. She took the lamp and a box of colored chalk back to her workspace.

As she sipped her orange juice, she read research articles and doctorial theses from JSTOR—short for Journal Storage—a digital library of academic journals. Her interests were in the latest developments in organic electronics.

After two hours, she leaned back and rubbed her eyes. She looked at the brick wall for a moment, then up at the dim light coming through the dirty skylight.

Next, she read a scholarly thesis for over an hour, trying to decipher the technical jargon. At lunchtime, she went to the kitchenette, and in the fridge she noticed several containers with names written on them.

"Don't touch anyone else's food."

The guy reached past her to take a pink Tupperware bowl with 'McGill' written on the side in black Magic Marker. He elbowed her out of the way to reach for a Snapple Peach Tea.

"Excuse *me.*" She stepped away from him.

Without replying, he took his bowl to the microwave. As his food warmed, he wrote 'Chunky Beef Soup' on the dry-erase board mounted on the wall where several other grocery items were listed.

He leaned back against the counter next to the microwave, folded his arms, and stared at Catalina.

His two-day-old beard was dark brown and neatly trimmed. His Persian blue eyes could have been cheering, had he let them. His longish hair was a shade lighter than his beard. Athletic and trim, he just missed being likeable.

She ignored him as she checked the freezer for something to heat for her lunch.

"Pissants eat Ramen Noodles." He glanced at the timer on the microwave.

Catalina took a packet from the freezer; 'Barbeque Beef and Rice.' She read the instructions.

"Seven minutes," he said when the microwave dinged.

"It says 'Five.'"

"It takes seven, Pissant." He took his hot food and cold drink, then brushed past her. "And clean up after yourself."

She watched him go to one of the cubicles.

Obnoxious Drone dick.

She set the timer for five minutes.

After taking a Snapple Straight Up Sweet Tea from the fridge, she sipped it while waiting for her lunch to heat.

The barbeque beef was barely warm after five minutes. She set the timer for two more minutes.

Rude Drone McGill. He could have been nice about it.

She returned to her desk, and while eating, she found an article on synthetic nerves.

As she read about an artificial nerve system developed for use with prosthetic devices, she clicked on the links to more research papers.

Her forgotten lunch grew cold as she studied tiny organic circuits printed on a person's skin.

Thirty minutes later, she was startled when her phone chimed.

"No phones!" someone shouted from behind her.

She turned to see several people glaring at her. The old man made a cutting motion across his neck.

After clicking her phone onto 'Airplane mode,' she answered the call.

"Hey, Cat. How's it going?" Marilyn, her roommate, asked.

"I'll text you," Catalina whispered.

"Why can't you talk?" Marilyn whispered also.

"Just text."

"Okay."

'I just pissed off all the Pissants again with the phone call,' Catalina texted to Marilyn.

'You can't use your phone in that stupid place?'

'Apparently not. Like everything else, I learn by being yelled at.'

'So, you got in?'

'Only for thirty days. If I produce something in that time, I might get to stay longer.'

'At least you're in.'

'Right.'

'I'm ordering pizza. Cecil, Mack, and Debbie are coming over. What time will you be home?'

'Don't wait up.'

'You ordering in?' Marilyn asked.

'No, they have food here.'

'All right. I'll see you when I see you.'

'KK.'

Catalina went back to her reading and found a post-grad student at MIT had used a 3-D printer to produce a human-like hand with synthetic nerves.

She was startled by someone standing beside her chair.

The redhead she'd seen in Victor's office stood staring at Catalina's computer.

Oh, God. Another obnoxious Drone.

"What's up?" Catalina asked. The redhead's dangling jade earrings held her attention.

"It's five after four, Saylor."

Catalina glanced at the lower right corner of her screen. "Yes, it is. Thank you." She stared at the redhead.

"You have an appointment with Mr. Templeton."

"Oh, crap!"

She scooted back and grabbed a notepad. The woman led her toward the door of Victor's office, opened it, then went in ahead of Catalina.

"Miss Saylor." Victor waved her to a chair in front of his desk.

The redhead took the chair next to her. She crossed her legs, adjusted her emerald green skirt, and positioned a note pad on her thigh.

"What do you think of this place so far?" he asked.

Catalina thought for a moment. "Hostility, rudeness, everyone is mean..." She glanced at the redhead. "Except for Joe."

"Yeah, he's a nice guy. Did you find everything you need?"

"I see we have printers, a scanner, and a copy machine, but no Three-D printer."

"Why do you want a Three-D printer?"

"I want to print a hand, and also some organic circuits." Catalina noticed from the corner of her eye the redhead looking at her, then the woman looked at Victor.

"What type of Three-D printer are we talking about?"

"A Dremel Three-D-Twenty."

The other woman wrote on her notepad. "How do you spell that?" she asked.

Catalina spelled it for her.

"What will you do with the hand and circuits?"Victor asked.

"The echolocation AI program I'm writing will need tons of data for machine learning."

"Yes, I suppose it will. What computer language are you using?"

"Python."

"Is it hard to learn?"

"Well, if you're familiar with Perl and Java, it's not too difficult."

"Hmm...I see."

"What's with the dorm rooms?" Catalina asked.

"Candidates with special circumstances will sometimes be assigned to a dorm room."

"Define 'special circumstances.'"

"After two weeks, if you're still here, we'll talk about that. In the meantime, I need your statements from the four credit card companies and any other past-due bills you have."

"They don't send paper statements anymore."

"But you can email them to me, right?"

"Yes."

"And your bank statement."

Catalina glanced at the redhead, who was taking notes again.

"Mr. Templeton," Catalina said. "Why do you need my financials?"

"Curiosity. Is it a problem?"

She shrugged. "I guess not."

"Is there anything else you need?" he asked.

"AWS Cloud Computing would be nice."

"Why do you need that?"

"My iPad won't be able to handle the data-crunching."

"We have a Power Edge T-Six-Thirty server."

"I used that to get online, but it's too old and slow. It would take a year to process one hour's worth of data."

"We'll discuss AWS after two weeks. Anything else?"

Catalina shook her head.

Victor opened a manila folder and removed some papers. He slid them across the desk.

"What's this?" Catalina asked.

"Our contract."

She flipped through the papers. "Eight pages?"

"No, just four. There're two copies."

After reading the first paragraph, she turned to page four and saw a place for her signature. He'd already signed his name.

"Take it home with you tonight and read it over. You can sign it tomorrow."

"And if I don't sign?"

"Then we can't help you."

She stared at the contract for a moment. "Can you give me the abridged version? Just the high points?"

"It says Qubit's Incubator agrees to provide a safe

and quiet workspace for you in exchange for five percent of the net profits, if any, from any product or idea produced during the term of this contract. You may receive other benefits as deemed necessary."

"It takes four pages to say that?"

"There's a lot of legal details. That's why I think you should take the time to read it before you sign you name."

"What if I never produce a marketable product?"

"Then we terminate the contract, and you're free to leave us, owing nothing."

Catalina held out her hand to the redhead, palm up.

"What?" the redhead asked.

"Your pen."

Catalina signed the first copy, passed it to Victor, then signed her copy.

"Okay." He placed the contract in the folder. "How's your workspace?"

"It's fine. A little bleak, but that's okay. What's the work schedule?"

He handed her a key card. "If you leave after six p.m., be sure the door is locked. I expect everyone to be here from eight to five, except Sunday and Sunday Plus One."

"Sunday Plus One?"

"We used to call it Monday, but we no longer have Mondays. On the day after Sunday, everyone comes in late and leaves anytime after two. Tuesday is the start of eight-to-five. Saturdays are casual, come in late, leave early. You're free to come in on Sunday if you want to."

"Okay. Do many people work late?"

"Most of the probationers put in a lot of time."

"Probationers?"

"You're here on probation for the first thirty days. I think probationers are called 'Pissants' out there." Victor tilted his head toward the bullpen.

"Yes, and the Drones get cubicles."

"They do."

"And Monarchs get upstairs offices?"

He nodded.

"How does a Drone become a Monarch?" Catalina asked.

"Receive a patent on an idea or device."

"A patent. Okay."

"Do you have to give that café..." He glanced at the redhead.

"Hugo's Blue Plate Special," she said.

"How did you..." Catalina began. "Nevermind."

"Do you have to give notice when you decide to quit?"

"It's just a phone call. I don't have to do anything like a two-week notice. Hugo can easily find someone to take my place."

"You should probably make that call today."

"All right." She stood. "I better get busy."

"Don't forget those financials."

Chapter Three

At 7:30 p.m., Catalina heated a cup of Ramen noodles.

"How you liking those noodles?" a slim Black guy asked as he took a glass bowl covered with aluminum foil from the fridge.

"Not bad," Catalina said. "I like them because they're quick and easy."

The microwave dinged, and she took out her steaming mug, while holding the door open for him. "Your turn, Drover."

He wrinkled his brow. "You know me?"

"Yes, and also your name is on the tin foil."

He laughed.   "Call me 'Alex.'" After removing the foil, he placed his bowl of mashed potatoes and gravy in the microwave.

"I'm Catalina Saylor."

"Really? Catalina is an island. How you spelling that last name?"

She spelled it.

"Cool play on words by your parents. An island and a sailor."

"Yeah, they were pretty cool."

He glanced at her but didn't ask about the word 'were.' "Whatcha working on?"

"Converting echolocation sound waves to tactile impressions."

"Holy crap."

"I know, and I have only twenty-nine days left to prove the concept. How about you?"

"I'm working on flexible solar cells," Alex said.

She sipped from her cup of noodles. "How flexible?"

"Like a cloth that could be made into clothing."

"Nice. I could take a walk in the sunshine and charge my dead phone at the same time."

"And your boyfriend's phone, too."

"Screw him," she said. "He can get his own charger."

"Ouch, harsh. What he do to you that's so bad?"

"He dumped me. I've got to get back to it."

"Yeah, me, too. I got seven days till I drop dead."

"You'll make it," she said.

The microwave dinged. "Later."

At the edge of the bullpen she noticed a large chalkboard on the wall next to a projection screen. It had a list of names, dates and information. Across the top was 'Patents Granted.'

The first one was Wayne Ponicar, Therapeutic Water Body.

Next was Dwight Calister, Stair Climbing Wheelchair.

Followed by several more names and their inventions.

When she walked back through the bullpen, she saw nine people still working.

As she ate at her desk, she watched a YouTube video of a prosthetic hand. She turned off the sound so she wouldn't get yelled at.

Halfway through her noodles, she began coding a new program.

When she leaned back to stretch her arms over her head, she realized it was after midnight. Swiveling around in her squeaky chair, she saw all the pissant desks were vacant. Through the doorway into one of the cubicles, she saw a guy working at his computer.

Drone dick McGill. Why are you still here?

She shrugged and turned back to gaze at her brick wall. After a moment, she stood, shoved her chair out of the way, then pulled the desk away from the wall.

She noticed McGill scowl at her when the screeching of the desk on the concrete floor caught his attention. She ignored him.

In front of her desk, she stared at the bricks for a moment, then opened her box of colored chalk.

Around 1 a.m., Catalina heard McGill make a lot of noise at his desk, apparently preparing to go home.

I guess he wants me to know he's leaving. Good riddance to an ugly annoyance.

She didn't turn to give him the satisfaction of knowing how irksome she thought he was.

It was after 4 a.m. when she went out through the side door, then checked to be sure it locked behind her.

* * * * *

Catalina got almost three hours of sleep, then rode her moped back to the Incubator.

With a cup of coffee and cream-filled donut from a Krispy Kreme box left over from the day before, she was back at her coding.

At 9:30, Joe came to her desk.

"You're drawing something on your wall," Joe

said.

Catalina looked at it for a moment. "Yeah, I started on it last night."

"What's it going to be?"

"Not sure yet. What's your project?"

"Telephoto glasses."

"Really?" She was quiet for a moment. "How do you control them?"

"It'll be a heads-up display on the inside surface of the glasses. Eye movement will turn it on and off, and operate the amount of zoom."

"I would love to have a pair of those," she said. "I could be on a road trip and zoom in on a mountain range in the distance without ever taking my hands from the wheel."

"Exactly."

"Cool idea."

"Thanks," Joe said.

"Who's that redhead?"

"Victor's assistant, Tracy."

"She's not very friendly."

"All business," Joe said. "Well, back to work."

* * * * *

In the outer office, Tracy pulled open her desk drawer. She picked up a dangly earring with an oval jade stone encircled in gold and slipped it through the hole in her left earlobe. When she looked for the second one, it wasn't there. She shoved aside pencils and paperclips but couldn't find it.

"What the hell?" she whispered as she opened another drawer.

At 3 in the afternoon, two workers wheeled a large crate up to the side of Catalina's desk. Without a word, they opened the box and removed bubblewrap.

Catalina grinned. *The 3-D printer!*

Tracy came to watch the men work.

They soon had the machine setup and plugged into Catalina's surge protector.

One of the men turned it on and ran some diagnostics, while the other man cleaned up the packing material.

Apparently satisfied all was in order, the guy handed a clipboard to Tracy. "Your signature, please."

Tracy signed the form, then traded the clipboard for a thick manual.

The two men took the crate and packing material and left the building.

Several people in the bullpen stared at Catalina, Tracy, and the new printer.

After Tracy gave the manual to Catalina and started for the outside office, one of the pissants asked, "Why does she get a Three-D printer?"

"Beats the hell out of me, Crammer." The door swished closed behind Tracy.

As Catalina read the manual, McGill came to examine the printer.

"Why do you get a Three-D printer?" he asked.

"It's not mine, McGill. It belongs to the Incubator."

"How can we use it when you have it way the hell over here?"

"It has Wi-Fi. If you'll get your crayons and a large poster board, I'll try to draw a picture of how a Wi-Fi peripheral device can be connected to a server. The drawing will be big and simple, something you might comprehend."

Joe laughed as he left his desk in the bullpen.

McGill turned to glare at Joe when he came toward them.

Joe smiled at McGill.

"I know how Wi-Fi works, Pissant," McGill snapped. "But why didn't they install it next to the server instead of way the hell over here?"

Catalina took a 32 gig memory chip that came with the instruction manual and plugged it into a slot on her iPad. "That's something you'll have to take up with Tracy." She flipped a page in the manual.

* * * * *

By 5 p.m., she'd installed the nylon filament roll that came with the printer and was ready to print the sample image from the memory chip.

As the printer hummed and nylon filament was pulled into the print head, a bright red object began to form.

Several pissants and two drones came to watch as layer upon layer built up on the bed of the printer.

"What is that?" someone asked.

Catalina shrugged as she watched.

"Some sort of statue?" another pissant asked.

"Maybe."

"It's a chess piece," Joe said.

Catalina smiled.

"A knight."

"Yeah," McGill said. "A knight."

It took only five minutes to produce the three-inch

tall knight.

Catalina cut it free from the printer bed, examined it, then handed it to Joe.

"Nice." Joe passed it to McGill.

"The edges are rough," McGill said.

"So?" Journey Covey, the Black woman who'd told Catalina to get out of the cubicle, took the knight from McGill. "Five minutes ago, it was just a coil of red nylon string."

"Can a Three-D printer print a Three-D printer?" Joe asked.

Everyone stared at him.

"Probably the outside parts," Catalina said. "But not the internal structure, or the electronics and coding."

"You could print all the parts," Journey said. "But you'd have to code the programming." She passed to knight to another drone.

"What are you going to print next, Catalina?" Joe asked.

Using her phone, she clicked a photo of him. "Your hand."

* * * * *

It was almost midnight when the last pissant left the building. All the drones and monarchs had left hours before.

Catalina went to the storeroom and took a spray bottle of Windex, along with a roll of paper towels.

She opened a back window and stepped out onto the fire escape.

After glancing around, she went up the metal stairs to the roof, then made her way along the parapet in the dark until she came to the skylight above her desk.

She looked down at her workspace for a moment, then at the bullpen and rows of cubicles.

It took a lot of Windex, and a half-roll of paper towels, but she finally cleaned away the years' accumulation of crud, leaving the glass sparkling in the moonlight.

* * * * *

The next morning at sunrise, she was back at her desk. The glow from above, cast her work area in a warm, yellow radiance. Turning in her chair, she saw the bright sunlight painting the far wall in golden orange while filling the whole place with beautiful natural light.

Just before seven, McGill came in and glanced about, smiling. When he saw Catalina watching him, he frowned. She duplicated his ugly grimace.

The brightened work area seemed to cheer everyone else as they came in, even old man Edison.

"When did they clean your skylight?" Joe brought his coffee and a spare chair to her desk.

"I have no idea." She grinned. "It was like that when I got here."

"You know..." He sipped his coffee. "That cleaning guy could have slipped and fell off the roof in the dark."

"Or he could have fallen through the skylight."

"Yeah, that would've made a mess on your desk."

"Uh-huh."

"Can you help me with something?" He sat in the chair beside her.

"I'll be happy to, if I can. But I know very little about optics."

"I've got the optics worked out. The power supply and the electronics are the problem. I can't have the users carrying a heavy box around on their backs.”

“What’s in the box?” Catalina asked.

“The circuit boards, a logic processor, and a twelve-volt motorcycle battery.”

“How big is the processor?”

“It’s basically a CPU chip to run the app,” Joe said.

“I think we can use the Three-D printer to print your circuits on thin polymer sheets.”

“Can you help me with that?” Joe asked.

“Sure.”

“Now I just need to get rid of that motorcycle battery.”

Chapter Four

Thursday morning, 9 a.m.

Victor came into his office. He stood for a moment, staring at the wall behind his desk.

Still looking at the wall, he yelled over his shoulder. "Tracy!"

"Yeah, Boss?"

"Come in here for a moment."

They stared at the wall, where an oval-shaped clean area decorated the wall behind his desk.

"I didn't take it," Tracy said.

"I'm sure it was there yesterday," Victor said.

She nodded.

"Who the hell would steal a picture of hieroglyphics?"

"An art thief?"

"Maybe."

"Did you ever figure out what the hieroglyphics meant?"

"No, but apparently someone else did."

* * * * *

At 10, Victor pushed open the door to the bullpen. "Show time," he said.

He was followed by Tracy, with her notebook and wearing one dangly oval earring.

"Joe," Catalina whispered, "what's going on?"

"Once a week—we never know when—Victor comes in for demonstrations of some of the projects."

"Holy crap. I'm not ready."

"If he calls on you, you have to show whatever you have."

A long stage ran along the front of the room. A projection screen, twelve feet wide, was attached to the wall behind the stage.

Victor stepped up on the stage. "Petunia Damien."

"On my way," came a female voice from the center of the bullpen.

Catalina watched the young woman adjust her hair, then grab her phone.

"Come on, Spittoonia," grouchy old Edison said. "I ain't gettin' any younger."

Petunia punched his shoulder when she passed by him.

He smiled.

On the stage, Petunia fluffed her auburn hair, then touched her phone.

Victor left the stage and took a chair beside Tracy.

Petunia turned her back on the bullpen as she continued tapping on her phone.

Everyone watched her and the projection screen. Maybe she was going to start a video.

37

"What the heck?" Catalina whispered.

"Look at her hair," Joe said.

Petunia's shoulder-length hair slowly began to lengthen in the back.

Murmured whispers came from the bullpen as her hair grew inch-by-inch toward her waistline.

Petunia turned to face her audience. She smiled as she took a lock of hair to hold it out in front of her.

The beautiful brown hair grew longer.

She glanced at her phone, then turned her back so everyone could see her hair was already down to her hips.

After tapping an icon on her phone, she shook her head, swishing the long strands from side to side.

Smiling, she turned back to the front. "That's it."

Catalina clapped, and soon the others also applauded.

"Good work," Victor said. "You can move into..." He glanced at something Tracy had written on her notepad. "Cubicle thirty-one."

As the happy Petunia went back toward her desk, a girl pissant stopped her to examine her hair. "Does it come in purple?"

"Any color you like, Norma."

"Roger Collingsworth," Victor said. "Are you ready?"

"Yes, sir." Roger took a pair of pink trainers from his desk and came forward.

On the stage, Roger said, "I need a lady volunteer with size seven feet."

Journey stood. "I wear size seven."

"Miss Journey," Roger said. "Come give me a hand—or foot, I should say."

A few people laughed.

Journey sat on the edge of the stage to pull on the

trainers and lace them.

She stood and stepped up on the stage. "Now what, Collingsworth?"

"Walk across the stage, then back this way." Roger stepped off the stage.

After a few steps, Journey said, "Well, they're comfortable."

"Keep going."

As she walked across the stage and turned, she smiled. "Hey, that's cool. When I start to lift my foot, the heel springs up. There's no effort at all. I'm almost floating."

At the end of the stage, she turned back. "Now it's starting to wear off, and I have to lift my feet."

"When you walk, energy is stored in a coil. When it's fully charged, it releases the energy, pushing the heel up. When the coil is fully expanded, it starts to tighten up again."

"Nice. Yes, now I feel the lift again." Journey stepped off the stage. "Can I keep these?"

Collingsworth grinned. "Sure, for only seven hundred bucks."

As she removed the trainers, he got a round of applause.

"Good work, Mr. Collingsworth." Victor whispered something to Tracy and studied a chart in her lap. "Move into cubicle twenty-three."

"Yes!" Collingsworth shouted. "Thank you, Mr. Templeton."

"You earned it." Victor looked around at the others. "Catalina Saylor, you're up."

Dang it. I'm not ready.

Catalina glanced at Victor.

He smiled and waved a hand toward the stage.

She took her iPad to the stage and logged onto the sever, then connected to the projection screen through her Wi-Fi.

A sketchy outline of a winged creature appeared on the screen. The lines became darker as the body became more distinct. The wings began to move as details filled in. A floating paintbrush, the type used by artists, appeared from the right side of the display. Black paint dripped from the tip of the brush as it advanced toward the creature, which turned its red eyes upon the approaching brush.

When the brush touched its chest, the animal, which was now clearly a bat, arched its wings upward as its chest expanded to receive the black paint.

The body was soon painted black, and the brush moved on to the wings.

When the bat was fully black, the brush withdrew and the bat took flight.

In slow motion, the bat rose in the moonlit sky, searching for prey.

Sound waves, shown as bright arcs emanating from the bat's mouth, spread out in a curved vertical array ahead of the flying creature.

For a time, nothing came back.

Then faint sound waves bounced back toward the bat's large ears as a weak sonar ping sounded from the speakers. The bat's ears perked up as it adjusted its course of flight.

Soon another flying creature appeared as the echoing sound waves bounced off its body and the ping increased in volume and frequency. The flying insect was a sphinx moth almost a third the size of the bat.

Without radar of its own, the moth fluttering through the dark night was unaware of the approaching predator.

When the bat was within a few inches of its victim, it made minute adjustments to its flight path in synchronization with the movements of the moth.

Just before impact, the bat arched its tail into a basket shape and scooped the sphinx moth from the air.

Still in flight, and while using its echo-location sound waves to avoid the surrounding trees, the bat doubled over to grasp the struggling insect in its jaws.

The bat clipped off the unnourishing wings and let them float toward the ground. It then began devouring the body, starting with its head.

The viewpoint of the CGI video drifted away from the dining bat to a man standing at home plate on a baseball diamond. He wore a blue surge suit, with a navy blue tie over a white shirt. His blindfold was red.

The man stood facing the pitcher's mound, where the pitcher wound up to throw a baseball toward home plate.

The blindfolded man held up his left hand, with the palm toward the pitcher.

When the pitcher threw the fastball, the blindfolded man shifted his body to the left and brought up his gloved right hand, catching the ball.

The computer-generated video froze on that final frame, with the man in blue holding the ball in his glove.

"So," McGill said, "the blue man used echolocation to catch a ball. So what?"

Catalina opened her mouth for a response, but a pissant spoke first. "Is this going to be another time-devouring video game?"

"The CGI is too jerky," another pissant said. "You have to make the movements smooth, like real movements of animals and people."

Catalina's shoulders slumped. She closed the lid of

her iPad, turning off the last frame of the video.

"You need some sort of sound for that last part. Maybe a fast-paced rock song; otherwise, it falls flat."

"Is there any practical use for this, or is it just a gimmick?"

She picked up her computer and left the stage. From the corner of her eye, she saw Victor and Tracy watching her.

"Adu Dhabi Wilson is next."Victor turned back to the assembled pissants and drones. "You're at T minus five days."

"Yes, sir."

Joe stepped onto the stage and placed his notebook computer and a large green box on the table. He opened his computer, connected the box to the computer's USB port, then connected his computer to the projection screen. He put on a pair of large glasses.

Two red wires ran from the temple of his glasses to the green box.

He flipped a toggle switch on the side of the box, and a blurred image appeared on the projection screen.

When he looked toward the screen, the projected image shifted that way.

Looking over the top of his glasses, he adjusted a control knob on the box. The image sharpened to a clear view of the floor.

Pushing up the glasses, Joe turned toward his audience.

The red wires pulled tight, yanking off his glasses. He caught them before they hit the floor.

Everyone laughed as a grainy view of his flustered face came on the screen.

"Gotta make those wires longer," he said as he put on the glasses.

"Or install a transmitter on your nose," McGill said.

More laughter.

"Yeah, I'm actually working on a transmitter."

As he stared at the pissants, their image came on the screen.

"Now, we do magic."

Joe touched the right side of his glasses, and the projected image enlarged and zoomed in on McGill.

The image wasn't perfect, but it was clearly the scowling face of McGill filling the screen.

Someone slapped McGill on the back. "Hey, you're on TV."

"So? He could do that with electronic binoculars from Amazon."

"But," Joe said, "you can't wear a pair of binoculars."

"And you can't walk down the street," McGill said, "with two short wires connected to a green box on wheels."

"I said I'm building a transmitter."

"Not in five days, you're not," McGill said.

Some of the others laughed, but Catalina applauded. "How'd you make the glasses zoom in, Joe?"

"Right now, I-I have a touch switch on the right temple, but there will eventually be a sensor to detect eye movement to control the telephoto."

"I'll buy the first pair when they're on Amazon." Catalina grinned at McGill.

Joe gave her a weak smile, then picked up his gear and left the stage.

"William Thomas Edison," Victor said. "You're at T minus ten days. Let's see your project."

Edison picked up his equipment from his desk and went to the stage. After placing the array of tubes and wires on the table, he went back to his desk for another item.

"This is a humidifier." He plugged it into the wall outlet. "The air conditioning in this place pulls most of the moisture out of the air, so I'm using the humidifier to simulate normal outside humidity."

He adjusted his apparatus. "Two billion gallons of water a day..." he said as a stream of moist air came from the humidifier and drifted toward his device, "...is lost to evaporation from Lake Nasser, in Egypt. The northeast trade winds carry this moisture over the Sahara Desert, where it doesn't fall as rain, as one might expect." He turned his array at an angle to catch the maximum flow from the humidifier. "Instead, the two billion gallons of water is lost to the upper atmosphere, where it eventually drifts out over the Atlantic Ocean, where it does fall as rain, exactly where it isn't needed."

As he spoke, small droplets of water began to form on the wires of his array. When the drops grew large enough, gravity caused them to drip into a collection tray.

"Abu Simbel is an ancient Egyptian monument on the edge of Lake Nasser. A city by that name has grown up around the stone edifice. Even though it lies on the edge of the lake, where all that water is being sucked up into the air, very little rain falls on Abu Simbel. Which is typical for any desert region, because perennial high pressure prevents rain clouds from forming."

"What good is that little bit of water going to do anybody?" McGill asked. "That thing has been running for five minutes and you've got two drops of water."

"This collection array has a surface area of one square meter," Edison said. "When it's scaled up to a hundred meters, it will provide a day's worth drinking water for one person."

"What's the population of Abu Simbel?" McGill asked.

"About twenty-six hundred."

"So, it would take a twenty-six thousand square meter net to catch enough water for the residents of Abu Simbel. And that doesn't count bathing and washing clothes."

Shut up, McGill. Catalina narrowed her eyes on him.

McGill looked at her, then shrugged.

"I think I can make it more efficient."

"It would be a lot cheaper to build a solar-powered water purification plant," McGill said. "To turn the lake water into drinking water."

Edison pulled the plug on the humidifier.

"I have a question," Catalina said.

"Yeah," Edison said. "What's that?"

"Why is the air so dry in a cooled area like this?"

"The moisture condenses on the coils of the air conditioning system and drips off to be drained away."

"Why does it collect on the coils?"

"They're filled with a coolant."

"So, when the compressor is turned off, no water vapor collects on the coils?"

"Right." Edison rolled up the cord on the humidifier.

"If your nanotubes were filled with a coolant, wouldn't they be more efficient in collecting water?"

"Sure, by a factor of about fifty times more efficient. But it takes power to compress and circulate the coolant."

"How about a heat pump powered by solar cells during the day and a flow battery at night?"

Edison looked at her. He didn't have an answer.

Everyone else stared at her, too.

"I'm just saying..." Catalina opened her iPad and clicked it on to do a Google search.

* * * * *

Late in the evening, when Catalina checked her email, she had a message from one of her credit card companies.

Oh, shit. Here goes my credit rating, right down the tubes.

She clicked on the message.

'Thank you for your recent payment. Your current balance is now zero.'

No way!

She had email messages from her other three credit card accounts as well; all paid off, as were her past due utility and insurance bills.

Yes! Thank you, Qubit.

* * * * *

At 5:45, Catalina turned in her chair to see Joe in the bullpen, staring at his green box.

She clicked off her computer and left her desk.

"Come on," she said.

"Where?" Joe looked up at her.

"You're going to buy me a drink."

From the corner of her eye, she noticed McGill roll back in his chair so he could see the two of them from his cubicle.

Joe stood and grabbed his jacket. "That's the best offer I've had all day."

Walking toward the door, she looped her arm in

his. "McGill's watching us," she whispered.

"Yeah, he's watching me walk out with a hot babe, and he's got nothing."

She giggled and reached to push open the door.

* * * * *

"It wouldn't be so bad if all the pissants hadn't piled on."

"Not all of them, Joe." She took a pull from her beer bottle and picked up a slice of pizza.

"Yeah. Thanks for being on my side."

Joe's hand began to shake. The bottle rattled on the table when he put it down. He picked up a slice of pizza, took a quick bite, and dropped it on his plate.

Catalina leaned toward him. "When something bad happens to you, it takes three good things to wash away that bad one."

He took hold of his bottle but didn't pick it up.

She put her hand over his. "You have to make those three things happen." She held up her empty bottle for the waitress to see.

"Yeah, three good things in five days."

"I'm going to help you with the printed circuits." She took away her hand.

He gulped his beer and reached for the fresh bottle the waitress had placed on the table.

"Tonight."

Joe stopped the bottle an inch from his lips and stared at Catalina.

She nodded. "Tonight."

He grinned and took a swig.

"You know Alex Drover?" she asked.

"Yeah, that skinny Black guy."

"He's working on a flexible solar cell."

"How would that help?"

"I think I might be able to sew a series of them into a lightweight jacket."

"Really?"

Catalina nodded. "For your next demo, you'll be wearing a new jacket covered with little silicone squares. And there'll be two red wires running from your telephoto glasses to the front of your jacket, then inside. I'll sew a pocket in there to hold your CPU chip, the printed circuits, and the connection to the inverter for the current from the solar cells."

"Will the cells work inside the building?" Joe asked.

"You know that clean skylight over my desk?"

"Yeah."

"At sunrise, the light shines on the far wall. Then, as the morning progresses, that square of sunlight moves down the wall, then across the bullpen, until at noon it disappears."

"So I need to do my demo between nine and ten to catch the best light."

"Right."

"All this in five days?"

"Absolutely," she said.

"You're going to burn five of your days to help me?" he asked.

"That's right. And after you move into your cubicle, you're going to help me with my project."

He clinked his bottle against hers. "Hell, yeah."

"I'll talk to Drover in the morning," she said. "I think he'll let me make a jacket for you because you can demonstrate his project at the same time you're doing yours."

Joe stared at her for a moment. "Catalina...I...um...have another problem."

"What?"

He unbuttoned his left cuff and pulled up the sleeve.

Catalina caught her breath. There in the crook of his arm was a series of needle tracks. Two were infected.

"Oh, no, Joe."

"I can't get through the day without a couple of hits. I've got a five-hundred-dollar-a-day habit."

"Damn it."

"I owe my guy over forty thousand." He stared at his beer. "And I'm totally broke."

Chapter Five

On Friday afternoon, Catalina heard the door open and turned to see a new girl come in.

Just as Catalina had been tossed into the bullpen, this young woman stood alone, staring at the jumble of desks.

She was the first new person since Catalina had arrived a week before. She felt a sense of relief that she'd no longer be on the bottom of the pile and treated by most of the pissants and drones as something less than a stray dog.

As the girl—who looked to be about Catalina's age, twenty-two—glanced around at the people staring at her, Catalina stood and went toward her.

The young woman smiled weakly, not sure of what would happen, especially with all the others either ignoring her or sneering, except for Joe.

"I'm Catalina." She held out her hand.

"Tafi Ari Rivo."

They shook hands.

"Did Victor tell you to come in and find a desk?"

Tafi nodded.

"I've only been here a week, and I got the same cold reception. What do you think of this desk?"

"It's fine."

McGill rolled back in his chair, staring at Tafi.

Tafi watched him as he glared at her. "Who's my boss? And please tell me it's him."

Catalina giggled. "No. He thinks he's king shit, but he's just the prince of squat. You're your own boss in this place."

Tafi put her purse on the desk. "So, I just work out here in the middle of this place?"

"This is called the bullpen, and yes, we start out here. If we're still here after thirty days, we get a cubicle and become a drone, like McGill."

"Victor told me I had thirty days to prove my concept. So, if he doesn't like my progress after the thirty days, I get kicked out?"

"I've seen three people leave in the past five days. They tell me the failure rate is almost eighty percent."

"Wow."

"I know. It's brutal. But if you make it and become a drone living in a cubicle, you've got a shot at a private office, up there."

Tafi looked where Catalina pointed. "Nice."

"That's where the Monarchs live."

"How do we get up there?"

"Receive a patent on your invention or idea."

"Are you going to be up there?" Tafi smiled at Catalina.

"I have to. This is the opportunity of a lifetime, and I plan to make the most of it."

"Good. I'll welcome you up there with me when you make it."

Catalina stared at her for a moment. "You know what? How about if we move this desk over there, next to mine?"

"Can we do that?"

"We can do whatever we want, but the other pissants won't like it."

"Did you say 'pissants?'"

"Yeah. Pissants are the people in the bullpen. You take that end, and I'll take this one."

When the metal bottom of the desk squeaked across the cement, old Edison yelled, "Knock it off."

Joe came to help them. "You two get on that end, and I'll take this end. I think we can work together and lift it."

"Thanks, Joe. This is Tafi Ari Rivo, our new pissant."

"Glad to meet you. I'm Adu Dhabi Wilson. Watch your feet."

"You want to face the wall, or the bullpen?" Catalina asked.

Tafi nodded toward Catalina's desk. "Like yours, facing the wall. Nice picture."

Catalina glanced at her brick wall. "Thanks." She'd added more detail, giving it depth and color.

"Jacket fitting tonight?" Joe asked.

"Yep. Did you get the new circuits wired up?"

"Almost." He fetched a chair from the bullpen. "Can you show Tafi the layout? I've got to get back to it."

"Sure."

Tafi tried out her chair, then checked the desk drawers; they were empty.

"I'll give you the tour," Catalina said, "and we'll get you some supplies."

In the supply room, Catalina asked, "What are you

working on?”

“Germ visualization.”

“With a microscope?”

“Sort of. The concept is that you would walk into a hospital corridor and see all the dangerous pathogens ahead of you.”

“Wow!” Catalina handed a tape dispenser to Tafi. “Sounds complicated.”

“Yes. All I have right now is the idea. The equipment is so expensive, I could never afford to buy it myself.”

“Stapler,” Catalina said, “and pencils.” She closed the supply room door.

“What’s in there?” Tafi asked.

“I don’t know. Let’s take a look.”

Catalina pushed the door open to find a huge open area. It was much like the bullpen, but empty except for layers of trash and dust on the cracked concrete floor.

“This whole place was some sort of factory,” Catalina said. “But I don’t think anyone’s been in here for years.”

They closed the door and started back toward their desks.

“What’s his name?” Tafi whispered.

Catalina glanced at the guy in the kitchenette. “That’s a Dick McGill.”

Tafi giggled. “I think I need a Coke.”

“Oh, my God. All right, come on.”

McGill ignored Tafi as he glared at Catalina.

“This is Tafi Ari Rivo. Tafi, meet McGill, our number one jerk and all-around never-nice-to-anyone drone.”

“Wonderful,” McGill said. “Another pissant to eat our food and use up the supplies.”

"Hi, Dick." Tafi's voice was weak and barely audible.

Catalina slapped her hand over her mouth to squash the laugh threatening to burst out. She turned to the fridge and took out a Coke and a Dr. Pepper.

"Is that the last Coke?" McGill asked.

"No, it's not the last Coke." Catalina grabbed the marker from the countertop and scribbled 'Coke' on the dry-erase board. "Now are your happy?"

"If it's not the last one, why write it on the board?"

"Because there's only one left in the fridge, McGill."

It didn't appear Tafi heard their heated words. She just smiled and watched McGill stir his coffee.

"Tell her to clean up after herself." He pushed between them. "Pissants are nasty."

"And that's McGill, the dick."

"He's kind of cute when he scowls," Tafi said.

"Well, then he's been cute since day one. Come on, I'll show you the rest of the place."

After the short tour, Tafi sorted her supplies and put them away.

"If you're all set," Catalina said, "I'm going to help Joe."

"Yep," Tafi said. "I've got all I need, but I think I'll go check out the snacks. And don't worry, I'll keep McGill happy and clean up after myself. Maybe he'd like a Twinkie to go with his coffee."

* * * * *

On Thursday afternoon, a week after Tafi came to the incubator, Victor and Tracy came into the bullpen to see how the projects were developing.

Three demonstrations went smoothly, then Victor called on Tafi for an explanation of her project.

While Tafi took the stage and checked the projection screen, Catalina pushed her chair over near the stage, clicked on her iPad, and used the Wi-Fi to connect to the server.

"The headline for my project theses is 'Visualization of viruses on a surface.'" Tafi glanced at Catalina, who nodded to her.

"Catalina coded a CGI presentation for me. So, as you watch the screen I'll explain my idea."

The video began with a large camera rotating left to right, then top to bottom, giving a nice all-around view.

"A Phase One XF IQ-Four One-fifty-one megapixel camera," Tafi said, "takes photos with the highest possible resolution available today. If someone took a picture of the Matterhorn from a hundred miles away with an XF IQ-Four..." a picture of the Matterhorn Mountain came on the screen, "...that photo could be enlarged to a point..." the photo clicked larger as the viewpoint slowly zoomed in, "...where individuals of a team of mountain climbers on Hornli Ridge could easily be made out."

Six climbers in orange jackets came into view and enlarged until they filled the screen.

"A photo taken with this camera, in a hospital corridor..." a long hallway with gurneys, electronic equipment, and nurses came into view, "...and then the digitized data delivered to a microsphere nanoscope..." a 360-degree rotating view of a Digital Instruments Atomic Force Nanoscope was displayed, "...could reveal objects, or creatures, as small as fifty nanometers in size.

"Viruses typically measure from ten to three hundred nanometers in diameter." Tafi glanced at the screen, where the photo of the nanoscope changed to a tiny magnified creature.

"Fifteen thousand individual coronaviruses lined up side-by-side would stretch across the head of a pin."

The ugly virus was duplicated and multiplied until thousands of them stretched across a curved, silvery surface.

"Fifteen thousand people standing shoulder-to-shoulder would stretch fifty-one miles, or about the length of thirty Golden Gate Bridges laid end-to-end."

The line of viruses morphed into a long line of people standing on the bridges.

"So, the scale of a pen head to a virus is as to thirty Golden Gate Bridges to a human." Tafi paused as the display moved back and forth between the viruses on the pinhead and people standing on the bridges.

"Using a microsphere nanoscope and artificial intelligence on a high-powered computer..." An image of a woman sitting at a table with the 151 megapixel camera, the nanoscope, and her computer, came into view. Behind the table was an array of blinking servers. "A program could be written to use the digital XF IQ-Four photo to identify the presence of viruses on a surface. This information could then be converted to a color-coded visual display overlaying the original photo of the hospital corridor, revealing the presence, or absence, of dangerous pathogens."

The original photo of the hospital corridor was smoothly overlaid with a color-coded image from the software, showing shimmering bright orange splotches on the floor, walls and table surfaces.

Tafi glanced at Victor, then turned toward the bullpen.

"Slapstick presentation with a half-baked video,"

McGill said, "that's all I see. How much does that camera cost?"

"Forty-nine thousand dollars," Tafi said.

McGill laughed.

"How much is the nanoscope?" Journey asked.

"Almost eighty thousand."

Another snort from McGill.

"Even with dense coding," old Edison said, "I don't see how you could walk around in a hospital with all that equipment."

"This is nothing but science fiction," McGill said.

"Most real science, McGill," Catalina said, "starts out as science fiction."

"Yeah, and most science fiction remains a fantasy because it's impossible to bring it to life."

"There was a guy..." Catalina turned her back on McGill and clicked off her iPad, ending the video, "...who, in eighteen-seventy, wrote a science fiction tale about a nuclear-powered submarine." She turned back to face McGill. "His name was Jules Vern. Perhaps you've heard of him. Only seventy years after the publication of *Twenty Thousand Leagues Under the Sea*, the USS Nautilus was launched. It was a real nuclear-powered submarine, with operating characteristics similar to the fictional Nautilus."

"Yeah, well," McGill said, "maybe in two hundred years we'll see color-coded germs crawling around before our eyes."

"Do you know the difference between eighteen seventy and today?" Catalina asked.

McGill shrugged.

"The technology needed for Tafi's project is already in existence."

"Mr. Templeton," McGill said. "Do we have to sit through any more comedy shows, or can I get back to work on an actual project?”

* * * * *

Tafi was in tears when she and Catalina returned to their desks.

“And that’s why we call him a ‘dick,’ among other things,” Catalina said.

Tafi slumped in her chair. “I thought it was a beautiful presentation.”

Catalina offered Tafi her tissue box. “You explained it perfectly.”

“You did a great job on the CGI.” She daubed her eyes.

“Now all we have to do is talk Mr. Templeton into spending a hundred and thirty thousand bucks,” Catalina said.

“Has the Incubator ever spent that much money before?”

“We need to talk to some of the monarchs to see how they got their projects off the ground,” Catalina said. “When I asked for that Three-D printer,” she nodded toward the printer beside her desk, “it was delivered the next day.”

Tafi glanced at the printer, then stared at the cubicles. “I’m going to get a Snapple for McGill.”

“Oh, my God.”

* * * * *

The next day, a bewildered young man came through the door and into the bullpen. He wore an ill-fitting gray suit, with a wrinkled white shirt buttoned tight at the neck. He carried a large, battered briefcase. His hair

58

was cut in a 1950s flat-top style.

He stood blinking at the twenty-four pissants glaring at him.

The poor guy seemed frozen to the cement floor.

Catalina caught Tafi's eye and smiled. She tilted her head toward the guy. "Your turn," she whispered.

Tafi grinned and went to greet the man.

Catalina watched them shake hands, then Tafi led him to their work area.

Tafi introduced him; Timothy Alexander.

"This is not what I expected." Tim set down his briefcase and wiped his brow with a handkerchief.

"Yeah," Catalina said. "They call it a bullpen for a reason. There's three vacant desks out there. Take your pick, and settle in."

"I'm not sure I want to be out there. It seems so hostile. Why are you guys over here by the wall?"

"We're outcasts," Catalina said.

"But we like it here," Tafi said, "away from the jerky pissants."

"Pissants?"

"Yeah," Tafi said. "We're all pissants until we get a cubicle and become drones, then later on, up there." She pointed up to the balcony. "Where the monarchs live."

Tafi and Catalina explained about the hierarchy.

"It must be really cool to be a monarch," Tim said.

"Yeah," the two women said together as they watched a guy come from one of the rooms and head for the stairway.

"What do you think, Tafi?" Catalina asked. "Shall we invite Tim to work over here, with us?"

"Heck, yeah," Tafi said.

"Heck, yeah," Tim said.

"All right. Let's go grab a desk and see if we can

piss off a few pissants."

After the desk made nails-on-chalkboard squeals on its way to their area, Tafi took Tim on a quick tour and helped him pick out supplies from the storeroom.

"What are you working on?" Tafi asked after she and Catalina pulled their chairs over to Tim's desk.

"Fake pangolin scales and meat."

"Pangolin?" Tafi asked.

"It's a small anteater native to Africa and parts of Asia, but ninety percent come from Sub-Saharan Africa. I need some modeling clay."

"I think there's some in the supply room," Catalina said. "They have scales?"

"Yes. The scales are sold to traditional doctors in China and Viet Nam, where they're cooked in boy's urine, then used to cure hysterical crying in children, excessive nervousness, women possessed by devils and ogres, impotence, malaria, and deafness, among other ailments."

"Girl's urine is no good?"

Tim nodded. "Probably something about testosterone. The killing and smuggling of the animas is a huge business in Africa."

"So," Catalina said, "they cook the scales in piss, then sell them?"

"Almost three million pangolins are killed by poachers every year in Africa. They're on the brink of extinction."

"Is there any science behind these cures?" Catalina asked.

"Yeah, voodoo science."

"Why don't the governments outlaw the poaching?" Tafi asked.

"Many countries have, but it's only served to drive up the prices and increase the killing of the gentle creatures."

"And you want to make fake pangolin scales?"

"Yes. Fake rhino horn is being produced and slipped into the supply chain. It's almost impossible to distinguish it from the real thing. And the fakes provide the same phony aphrodisiac effect as the real thing. It's like a placebo."

"Interesting."

"Pangolin meat is also highly prized, especially in Viet Nam, where it sells in restaurants for as much as a hundred and fifty dollars a pound."

"Wow," Catalina said. "No wonder they're being wiped out." She glanced at his desk. "If you're all set, I need to go help Joe."

Chapter Six

Friday, 5:30 a. m.

Catalina put away her chalk and stood back, admiring the wall.

A colorful monarch butterfly with a woman's body stood on a banister, leaning forward, ready to take flight. Behind the monarch was a row of doors, all closed except one. Inside that room could be seen a chrysalis hanging from the ceiling. It was split open and empty.

When the others started coming in at seven, she heard murmurs, but she ignored them as she worked on the coding for the tactile interface module of her program.

Tafi came to her desk at 7:30. "Wow, Catalina. It's beautiful."

"Thanks."

"Is that a chrysalis?"

"Yes, as if the butterfly had just emerged from its metamorphosis."

"That woman looks familiar."

"Really?" Catalina gazed at the picture for a moment. "How about some breakfast?"

                    * * * * *

    "Tafi," Catalina said, "do you have a triple-A battery?"

    "No, sorry. What died?"

    "My little penlight." She glanced around at the workers in the bullpen; they looked very busy. Her eyes then fell on McGill, in his cubicle.

    "I bet that doofus has one." She left her desk and crossed the bullpen.

    "Hey, McGill, you have a—" She stopped at the entrance to his cubicle, staring.

    A black device, twelve inches long and an inch wide, lay on his desk. As she watched, a tiny stream of gray smoke came from an aperture near the end. Before the smoke was an inch high, a second stream came from the next opening, then a third. Within twenty seconds, two dozen streams of smoke rose to form a translucent cloud, rising higher and higher.

    The faint scent of peach and apricot blossoms filled the cubicle, as if from a smoldering incense stick.

    McGill placed a small black pyramid near the edge of his desk, in front of Catalina and facing the smoke. When he touched a key on his iPad, the Beach Boys' *Fun, Fun, Fun* came from four speakers spaced out along the back of his desk.

    With the first beat of the music, a spherical beam came from the top of the pyramid and painted a blurred image on the smoke. The image began to writhe and come into focus.

    "Holy cow," Catalina whispered.

    The image sharpened as it moved to the music. Soon it became a girl of about four years dressed in cheerleader uniform, keeping perfect time with the song.

The frequency of the sound increased little by little until it exceeded the audible range and slipped into the ultra-high dimension.

Catalina could no longer hear the music, but the girl continued to dance.

The UHF waves vibrated the molecules of the smoke, setting them into a synchronized rhythmic 3-D motion, keeping time with the girl and music.

Not only did the sound waves move the smoke, they penetrated Catalina's clothing and soothed her skin and muscles.

"That feels like...a dozen soft hands..." She closed her eyes as her mind slipped into an almost hypnotic state. Mesmerized, she tried to speak again. "A dozen soft hands...massaging my tired muscles. I could just...drift..."

The taste of freshly sliced peaches touched her tongue.

The tingling and taste faded. She opened her eyes to see the little girl bow, as if to an admiring crowd in a theater.

Smoke stopped coming from the black device, and the remaining gray-blue cloud rose and began to dissipate.

Catalina watched the last of it disperse into the air above his cubicle.

"Wow," she whispered. "That was like being in a Jacuzzi at sunset. Just floating away with a glass of Andre peach wine and..."

Reality brought her back to McGill's face. "I need a triple-A battery."

"That's it? That's all you've got to say?"

"I said, 'Wow.' What more do you want?"

"Oh, I don't know, maybe 'Good work, McGill.'"

She patted him on the head. "You're such a good boy." Her smile was completely over the top. "Someday I'll bring you a chew toy. Now, give me a sucking battery."

* * * * *

Just after three in the afternoon the door from Victor's office opened, Catalina, Tim, and Tafi turned to see a new guy of about thirty-five stride in. He held an old-fashioned leather briefcase in one hand and armload of textbooks in the crook of his arm. He also carried a furled black umbrella.

He glanced around at all the pissants glaring at him, then, seeing the cubicles, he marched through the bullpen toward a vacant one.

Catalina and the other two jumped up to intercept him.

"Hold on, Hotshot," Catalina said.

"You're not quite there yet," Tafi said.

"What are you people jabbering on about?" he asked in a very crisp British accent. "Mr. Templeton said to come in, pick a desk, and take possession."

"Yes," Tim said. "But he was talking about one of these out here." He swept his hand toward the bullpen.

"Bloody hell," he whispered. "How bleak."

"Exactly," Catalina said. "Come on, we'll buy you a cup of coffee and give you a quick education on the Incubator."

"Gag. Please, not coffee."

"A soft drink?" Tafi asked.

"I don't suppose you have tea?"

"Iced or hot?" Catalina asked.

"You have got to be joshing me." He accentuated his accent.

"I say," Catalina said, "I do believe the chap prefers hot tea."

65

That got a laugh from him.

In the kitchenette, Tafi put on the kettle, then joined the others at a small round table.

"I'm Lucius Pritchard," he said.

The other introduced themselves, then explained how the Incubator was organized.

"Am I to assume the three of you are pissants?"

"Yep," Tafi said, "on our way to becoming cubiclized drones."

Catalina stood to go attend to the whistling teapot, then brought back a cup with a Lipton teabag tag hanging over the side. She also carried the steaming kettle, a Coke, a Snapple, and an orange juice.

"Hmm," Lucius said, "a teabag. How American." He poured the hot water.

"That's us," Tim said.

"I knew I should have secreted a packet of Earl Grey leaves for this little foray into an intellectual desert."

"I could listen to you talk all day long," Tafi said. "I love your accent."

"Yes," Catalina said, "me, too. But I think we've just been insulted."

"Not at all." Lucius sipped his tea. "To the attentive ear, that would be known as the famous British dry wit."

"Dry is right," Catalina said. "How do we get a nickname out of 'Lucius Pritchard'?"

"My lab mates call me 'Professor Pritchard.' Behind my back, I believe the preferred nick is 'Pritch the Bitch,' but I like the pet name my bride of fifteen years calls me, 'Lew.'. Her name, by the way, is 'Katharine,', or the more genial 'Kat.'"

"Lab?" Tim asked.

Lou sighed before he answered. "I recently

resigned from a very secure, well-paid position at the RNA Institute, part of the University at Albany. I have now cast my fate upon the capricious whims of the so-called bullpen and its strange inhabitants."

"What part of England did you come from?" Tafi asked.

"My father's people came from Basingstoke. My mother was born in Hyderabad, India. She was trained as a nurse at the University of Delhi. She immigrated to England and met my father in a tawdry pub in Barking. I have no idea what either of them were doing in that depraved part of London."

"What's your project?" Tim sipped his orange juice.

"A strawberry tree. This tea is offal." He shoved the cup toward Catalina and took her Coke. "Yes, I said 'offal.'"

Catalina tried the tea, made a sour face, then added a pink packet of sweetener. "I'm visualizing a tree with low-hanging branches where one could pluck ripe red berries as she walks under the limbs."

"And figs." Lew sipped the Coke.

"Okay, now I'm intrigued," Tafi said. "Give us the one-minute summation, and we'll decide if you'll be allowed to become one of the Outliers."

"I'm not sure I want to join a group who label themselves as outcasts, but here's the abridged edition of my proposed project; a hybrid plant created by crispr gene editing using deoxyribonucleic acid from two intrafamilial plants, i.e., the ground-dwelling strawberry plant, *Fragaria ananassa,* and the epiphyte strangler fig, *Ficus aurea.*"

"And in English," Tim said, "that would be?"

"He's going to snip out parts of a fig tree DNA,"

Catalina said, "and replace that gap with DNA from a strawberry plant."

"Isn't that what I just said?"

Tafi laughed. "Okay, Lew, I think my two pals will agree with me in inviting you to join our little band of outlaws."

"Against my better judgment," he held out his hand, "I'm officially accepting."

All three of them joined their hands with his.

"Okay," Catalina said, "let me take care of this." She scooted back her chair, then went to the dry-erase board, where she added to the grocery store list; 'Earl Gray tea leaves,' underlining 'leaves.' "Now, let's go steal a desk from the bullpen and drag it to our little penal corral."

During a lunch of sandwiches at their desks, Tafi ran Catalina's video of the bat catching a moth and the blindfolded guy catching a ball.

"Very nice," Lew said. "I'm guessing that's CGI. Who did the coding?"

"That would be your pissant pal, Catalina," Tim said.

Catalina smiled and bowed her head slightly toward Lew.

"Congratulations on a superb presentation," Lew said. "What are your plans for dinner?"

"Not a date with you," Catalina said.

"Then how about a date with me, my wife, and a pernicious teenage Goth daughter?"

"What's for dinner?"

"Hold on one sec." Lew took out his cell, but before he could click a button to make a call, Catalina grabbed his hand.

"Texting only, and put it on silent mode," she said. "Otherwise, you'll have half the bullpen down on our necks.”

“Hmm. All right.” He clicked out a message. “I’m just checking with my housemate before I make any commitments about our evening’s repast.”

“Good idea,” Tafi said.

Soon, Lew phone’s vibrated.

“So, my lovely wife has approved of our friendly engagement, and she will be giving us roast beef with *tikka masala* curry at approximately seven p.m.”

“Sounds...interesting,” Catalina said. “Should I bring wine?”

Lew clicked out a message. He smiled when the message pinged back. “I have been informed that Budweiser Chelada is the preferred adult beverage to accompany the *tikka masala.*”

“Okay. And what for the Goth girl to drink?”

“Who knows. I’m sure she would go for a Bud, but that’s not going to happen, at least not at her mother’s table.”

* * * *

At dinner that night, Catalina was introduced to Lew’s family.

“Katrina,” Lew said to his wife, “this is Catalina Saylor.”

“I am so glad to meet you. Please, call me ‘Kat.’”

She was a slender, dark woman in her late thirties, with a bright, engaging smile.

“And this is our daughter, Matilda.”

She was almost as dark complected as her mother, but there was no smile.

“It’s ‘Morticadi,’ Lucius,” the teenager said.

“Oh, pardon me. I had forgotten we named you

for the Goddess of

Gothic rituals. And my name, by the way, is 'Dad.'"

"Yes, we named you after the God of Tedium." She glared at her father, then turned her withering look upon Catalina, as if daring her to say something.

Morticadi could've been a beautiful teen girl except for the silver nose ring, black lipstick, coal-black mascara, and black circles under her cold gray eyes. Black blush on her cheeks completed her sickly, skeletal appearance.

Catalina's phone came to life and played the first few bars of *Oxytocin*, by Drab Majesty.

Morticadi's eyes widened as she stared at the phone.

Before arriving on her moped, Catalina had set her phone app to ring her every five minutes, in case she had to make an escape. She'd also added a few Goth songs to her ringtones.

Catalina glanced at the girl, then answered her cell. Of course, no one was there, but she pretended to talk to someone.

"Oh, no. I forgot all about it." She waited a beat. "I'll be there as soon as I, um, as soon as I can." She rang off.

"Sorry." She laid her phone face-down on the table. "Kat, this curry is deliciously hot. What's that spice?"

"It's Kashmiri pepper, along with *Bhot Jolokia*, or ghost pepper, as it's called here in the states. Tell us about Qubit's Incubator."

"The Incubator is a place where one can work on a project undistracted by life's little problems, like past-due bills or noisy office mates. It's very difficult to enter the program. Victor Templeton, the manager, said only two percent of applicants are accepted and eighty percent of those drop out before the end of their thirty-day probationary period."

The girl, apparently bored with the conversation, chewed a bite of food and began texting.

"Pissants," Lew said.

His wife and daughter looked at him.

"That's what they call the probationers. If you can demonstrate a feasible product or idea before the end of the thirty days, you're invited to stay on, and also allowed to move into a cubicle, to become a drone, on your way, hopefully, to graduating into a monarch."

Kat poured more beer into her glass. "That first thirty days sounds hectic."

"It is," Catalina said as she cut a bite of roast beef. "Very tense and combative. Only four or five drone slots open up each month."

"Kat," Lew said, "you've got to see some of the CGI presentations Catalina has coded for the other pissants."

"I know your plant grafting idea will work," Kat said to her husband, "but how can you convince–"

Morticadi interrupted her mother. "How many days till you're kicked out?" she asked Catalina.

Catalina sipped her Budweiser as she watched the girl's steady gaze. "I've got twelve days left."

Catalina's phone played *The Future is Black,* by Sonsombre.

Morticadi stared at her as she took another fake call.

"Why do you have Goth ringtones?" Morticadi asked when Catalina put down her phone.

"I like 'em, as well as Country and Western, Beethoven..."

The girl pushed back her chair and stood. "You wanna see my room?"

"Um..." Catalina glanced at her hosts.

Lew shrugged, and Kat smiled.

"I guess so." She took another bite of curry and grabbed her Bud to take with her.

Upstairs, Morticadi pushed open the door and waved in Catalina.

"Holy freakin' smokes!"

The girl closed the door behind her.

"I've...I can't..."

Catalina gazed around the room, trying to take it all in at once. She walked slowly toward a shelf above the TV. Her hand stopped halfway to an object. She looked over her shoulder at Morticadi.

The girl nodded her permission.

When Catalina took the beautiful object, a ring, from the shelf, she slipped her hand into the pocket of her skirt. She took out one of her keepsakes and handed it to the girl.

"Oh, my God!" Morticadi said, smiling for the first time.

Catalina fondled the turquoise gemstone ring. The blue-green translucent stone shimmered in its solid gold oval setting as she slipped the ring onto her little finger. It was too large, so she moved it to the third finger of her left hand.

"Blow..." Catalina said as she turned it in a circle, trying to take it all in.

"Blow?"

"This must be what a blow..." She handed her beer to Morticadi and walked across the room to a nightstand, where a dozen objects were arranged in an oval pattern. "What a blow job feels like."

The girl laughed and drank from the bottle. "Or cunnilingus."

"No, not even close." Her phone chimed. Without looking at it, she turned it off.

"Evangeline Psychiatric Hospital," Morticadi read from Catalina's oval nameplate. "There's got to be a great story behind this."

Catalina didn't respond. Leaving the ring on her finger, she reached for a carved ivory locket on a silver chain. Using her thumbnail, she clicked the small silver clip, popping the locket open into two perfect oval halves. In the right side was a tiny portrait of a young boy. Facing him, in the other oval, was a woman dressed in a high-necked Victorian dress.

She looked closer and touched the boy with a fingertip. "These aren't photos."

"No, they're hand painted miniatures," Morticadi said.

"This belongs in a museum."

"Yes. It did."

"One, two, three..." Catalina began counting.

"There's a hundred and fifty-four."

Catalina smiled at the girl. "I have two hundred and twelve."

"And not a single one paid for?"

"Absolutely. If they're bought, they're worthless."

"Right." Morticadi ran her finger around the edge of Catalina's nameplate. "I've never met another klepto oval maniac before."

Catalina laughed. "Me either. This is so cool. Do you think there are more of us out there?"

"They're proly all locked up in Evangeline Psychiatric Hospital."

"No," Catalina said. "Those people are all totally nuts."

"And we're not?"

"I don't think we're crazy; just possessed."

"No, we're bat shit crazy. Can I trade you something for the nameplate?"

"I bet you have something in here you wouldn't trade for love nor money."

Morticadi went to a shelf in the corner of her room, next to her bed. Upon the oak shelf was a carved wooden box, standing upright. She opened the two doors of the box, and as she did so, a tiny concealed golden light came on, illuminating the interior like a shrine. She reached for an object measuring about four inches long by three inches wide, and made of hardened pink clay. It was, of course, a perfect oval. She handed it Catalina.

"Wow. A baby's footprint." She looked into the girl's eyes, now softened, but not quite teary. "Yours?"

She nodded. "I was an hour old."

"This is what the oval nameplate means to me," Catalina said. "It's sacred."

Morticadi nodded, took the footprint, replaced it in its shrine, and closed the doors.

"What do you have," Catalina went to a bookshelf, where there were a few books, but mostly ovals, "that you'd trade for one of mine?"

Morticadi stood beside her, glancing along the shelf at her treasures.

Suddenly, they heard a knock at the door and jumped away from each other, as if they'd been caught having sex. Morticadi dropped the empty beer bottle on the floor.

The door opened, and her parents came in.

"You've been up here for almost an hour," Lew said.

"We thought you'd been kidnapped," Kat said.

"No," Morticadi said. "We were just listening to

some Goth tunes.”

Lew and Kat glanced at the silent iPad, where Morticadi’s music was stored.

“I thought we were going to talk about animating your project?” Catalina said to Lew. She knelt to pick up the beer bottle.

“Yes, that was my evil plan when I invited you to our humble home.”

“Well, let’s get to it,” Catalina said.

Morticadi caught Catalina’s arm as her parents left the room. She held out her hand, palm up.

“Oh.” Catalina slipped the ring off her finger and handed it over. “Force of habit.”

Morticadi smiled and returned the nameplate.

“You want to take a ride on my moped after your dad gets animated?”

“Hell, yeah. I’ll pick out a couple of items to trade before we leave.”

At the dinner table, they ate the food Kat had warmed in the microwave, while Catalina and Lew talked about his upcoming presentation.

It was almost midnight when Morticadi came down from her room and announced she was going home with Catalina.

Her parents, apparently accustomed to their rebellious daughter’s attitude, nodded their permission.

“Tomorrow’s a school day,” Kat said.

“I’ll see that she gets home soon,” Catalina said. “And tomorrow morning, Lew, I’ll need some specs on that strangler fig tree.”

* * * * *

Morticadi had to examine each of Catalina’s two

hundred and twelve ovals and hear the stories behind them.

They were as a pair of twins suddenly reunited, never having known of each other's existence.

Morticadi lay on Catalina's bed, supporting her head on her left hand. On the flowery bedspread, she placed the two ovals she'd brought from her collection for trade. "Do you realize," she said, "we have three hundred and sixty-six ovals, and not a single duplication?"

"Yes." Catalina picked up the oval bracelet made of silver and engraved with intertwining grape vines. Slipping it on her wrist, she touched the filigree etching along the edges. "Beautiful."

The other item was polished opal on a gold chain. Catalina placed it around her neck and positioned the stone between her breasts.

"I love it."

She rolled off the bed and went about her room, picking out a dozen objects. She spread them out before Morticadi, then lay on the bed, facing her.

"Take any two you like."

Morticadi smiled. Then, as she touched each item, she glanced at Catalina.

Catalina maintained a somber expression, refusing to show any emotion connected to the pieces.

The girl picked up a brass belt buckle displaying a cowboy on a bucking bronco.

"No!" Catalina cried and buried her face in her hands.

"Oh, shit. I'm sorry."

Catalina pulled away her hands and laughed. "Gotcha."

"You bitch!" Morticadi shoved her shoulder, pushing her off the bed. "Hey." She leaned over the edge of the bed, looking down at Catalina. "Let's practice."

They spent the next hour wandering about the room, one pretending to be an inattentive store clerk, while the other lifted various items and hid them up their sleeves, in their hair, their bras...

"When's your first class?" Catalina slipped a single jade earring into the waistband of her jeans, behind her back.

"Eight-thirty, trig." Morticadi glanced at the shelf. "Hand over the earring, you freaking amateur."

"Let's go get some breakfast, then I'll drop you off."

Chapter Seven

Early Tuesday morning of the following week, Victor and Tracy came into the bullpen.

"Mr. Lucius Pritchard," Victor said as he and Tracy took the two chairs near the end of the stage, "let's see this wonderful bi-fruit tree of yours."

"Catalina," Lew whispered, "I'm nowhere near ready to do this."

"He's not going to expect a completed project after only a week," she said, "but you have to show what you've done so far."

She'd been so intrigued by Lew's project, she'd burned through five of her project-days, coding the demo for him.

"My CGI code isn't complete," she said. "It's still rough around the edges, and the last segment isn't finished. But you go up there and start talking, while I set up the video."

"All right, here goes."

As Lew took the stage, Catalina pushed her chair over near Tracy. She sat, connected to the server, and lit up the projection screen.

"The problem with lab rats like me," Lew spoke to the assembled pissants and drones, "is that they are seldom allowed into the light of day to communicate with real people."

That earned him a few laughs.

He glanced up, looking toward four monarchs watching from the balcony.

After glancing toward Catalina and getting a smile and nod, he continued.

"This is a fable about the strangler fig and the wasp. A story of incest and co-evolution.

"The Florida strangler fig (*Ficus aurea*) and the wasp (*Pegoscapus mexicanus*), an insect so rarely seen that it has no common name, are so tightly co-evolutionized that if one of the pair ceases to exist, the other would also wither and disappear from the face of the Earth."

The screen behind Lew came to life as a wasp flew across a desert landscape.

"This marriage of two different species is akin to a woman (*Homo sapiens*) cohabitating with a strawberry plant (*Fragaria ananassa*) inside an isolated environment. This theoretical place, perhaps a remote desert oasis known as Strawbericaria, has only the woman, the strawberry, and water."

As the wasp came to rest at the edge of a blue pool of water, it morphed into a young woman wearing shorts and a tee. She sat beside a strawberry plant.

"The difference between Strawbericaria and the environment of the strangler fig tree is that the fig and the wasp aid each other in propagating their separate species."

The woman cupped her hand in the water, then dripped the water over the plant. The strawberry plant visibly responded by rising its leaves to reveal a single ripe strawberry. The woman plucked the red berry and bit into it while cultivating the sand around the plant with her fingers.

"The residents of Strawbericaria, sadly, are doomed to oblivion. They can provide nourishment for each other, but they cannot help pollinate one another for the purpose of reproduction. They may happily grow old together; however, their lines end with their death.

"We may never know how the wasp and the fig came to their arrangement of a life of monogamy—the practice of having a sexual relationship with only one partner—but it has been a successful marriage since long before the hairy ancestors of *Homo sapiens* first set foot on the ground.

"The life cycle of these two biologically separate species begins when the fruit of the fig tree flowers internally and provides an opening almost large enough for the female wasp to enter."

The image behind Lew now changed to the hollow interior of a fig. A shaft of sunlight came into the fig through a narrow opening.

"She is so determined to enter the fig that she sheds her wings and antenna in order to reduce her size enough to squeeze inside, where she will remain for the rest of her life.

"However, she is so happy to enter this cozy, safe environment that she spreads pollen, brought with her from her natal fig on another tree, from a specialized pouch on her abdomen as she lays her fertilized eggs on the fig's enclosed flowers. The opening where she entered slowly closes tight, entrapping her forever."

Lew glanced over his shoulder to see the video was perfectly synchronized with his delivery.

"Once this task of pollination is complete, the female wasp dies and is ingested by the fig.

"When the wasp eggs hatch, the males and females mate. Yes, this is the incest part; they are brothers and sisters.

"After mating, the male's only job is in gnawing an exit for his pregnant sister. He soon dies, and she happily departs with her collection of fig pollen and fertilized eggs, to find a home in a different strangler fig tree.

"Once the wasps have completed their part of this relationship, the fig ripens and is eaten by birds and other animals.

"The fig seeds are deposited with the diners' excretion, hopefully in the moist crotch of a tree unrelated to the fig.

"In that fertile environment, some of the seeds will sprout and send their branches toward the host's canopy to gather sunlight while it sends roots down the trunk of the tree toward the ground.

"As these strong roots seek moisture from the earth, they encircle downward and squeeze the tree trunk, thereby strangling the life from it, leaving nutrients in the soil for the fig plant to utilize in producing fruit for the wasp to move into. Thus beginning the cycle anew.

"The strawberry tree I'm working on is a intrageneric, or intrafamilial hybrid plant that produces figs and strawberries.

"Normally, intrafamilial plant grafts are universally unsuccessful. However, with genetically engineered species of strangler fig tree and strawberry plants having their DNA altered by the process known as crispr gene editing, they can be hoodwinked into believing they are indeed one in the same plant."

Catalina interrupted the presentation. "I'm sorry, Lew. That's as far as I got on the CGI programming."

Lew turned to see the paused image of the strawberry tree, where a boy and girl were reaching for the fruit.

"You've done a wonderful job on this," Lew said, "and I think you deserve a round of applause for not only a superb video, but also for using five of your project-days to produce it."

Everyone clapped and cheered for Catalina.

She stood and bowed to the crowd.

"Good work," Victor whispered.

"Thank you," she said, then spoke to Lew. "I'll leave that last frame on for you."

"Okay, good. Now," he said as he turned back to the audience, "once this new strawberry tree is in healthy production, two additional artificial evolutions take place.

"The first is solar cell leaves designed to harvest sunshine and convert it to a nourishing tree sap to augment the fig tree's natural source of food.

"The next is root sensors connected to a processor chip embedded in the tree's trunk. This processor, powered by a portion of the solar cell leaves and a flow battery, will continually monitor the moisture and nutrient content of the soil and automatically add these elements as required. Artificial intelligence code will feed water and enriched liquid nourishment from centralized storage facilities located within the orchard through dedicated piping."

Lew looked once more at the tree behind him, then said, "That's all I have for now."

Just when several people began to clap their hands, McGill held up his hand for silence.

"I must say, this has been a very cute presentation," McGill said, "especially with the Disneyesque mini movie's attempt to distract us from reality, but seriously, this is, as you said at the outset, nothing but a fable. Any schoolboy could poke several holes in the pseudoscience you've presented."

"Such as?" Lew folded his arms, staring at McGill.

"Oh, where to start," McGill said. "So many insurmountable scientific roadblocks, it's hard to choose one."

"Try your best," Lew said.

"All right. Interspecies grafting. You flew right past that with about three words. This is akin to mating a granite boulder with a beach ball, neither of which is aware of the other's existence, let alone any knowledge of the reproductive process. And you spent even less time explaining a complex, and so far as I know, unproven process of converting sunlight into tree sap. And you completely overlooked the process of changing a nepiphyte..." McGill glanced at the others, "that's an air plant to you people, like an orchid, almost a parasite living off   another—"

"Oh, shut up, McGill," Catalina said. "Just because you can't come up with any original ideas, you have to display your arrogance by cutting other people down."

"Original ideas?" McGill said. "You mean like your pipedream of blind people playing soccer with quadrupeds?"

"Yeah, I guess we could probably find four Nikes for you to wear. But in the meantime, you should remember these first demos are preliminary presentations of a thesis, not of a *fait accompli*. That means something that's already happened."

"No shit," McGill said. "You know what, I—"

"All right, kids," Victor said, "moving on to Tim's project."

Catalina and McGill continued to glare at each other as Tim took the stage.

Chapter Eight

The next day, at mid-morning, Catalina heard the office door open. She turned to see Victor and Tracy come into the bullpen. They were followed by two men in suits, along with two uniformed cops, one of which was a woman.

Tracy pointed toward Catalina. "That's her."

"We'll take it from here." One of the men—a big guy in a gray suit—came toward her. The other three followed close behind.

"Catalina Saylor?"

"Yes."

"Stand and step away from your desk, please."

She did as she was told.

The big guy motioned for the woman cop to come forward.

"Hold your hands away from your body," she said. "I'm just going to check you for weapons and contraband."

"Weapons?"

"Quiet, please." The woman patted her down.

At Catalina's desk, the man in the gray suit pulled on a pair of blue medical gloves and opened the middle drawer.

Tafi stood and stepped away from her desk, standing next to Tim and Lew. Everyone in the bullpen watched as the cubicles emptied out and several people came from the upstairs offices to lean on the banister.

"She's clean, sir," the female cop said.

The man, who was apparently a detective, nodded as he searched through her desk.

Catalina watched Joe when he dropped into his chair and pushed himself behind old Edison.

The detective pulled out the lower right drawer and searched through the contents. In the back, he found a rolled-up red scarf. He laid it on the desktop and unrolled it. He stared at something for a moment, then held out his hand to his right. "Evidence bag."

Catalina exhaled a sigh as she dropped her chin to her chest.

The other cop handed the man in gray a plastic zipper bag.

After the detective bagged the items, he turned around. "Catalina Saylor, you are under arrest for trafficking in illegal and controlled substances. You have the right to remain silent..."

The female cop cuffed Catalina's hands behind her back.

"Bag her phone, Mike," the detective said as he started for the door.

The other cops followed, with the female cop holding Catalina with a firm grip on her biceps.

* * * * *

At Midtown Precinct South, Catalina was booked, photographed, and fingerprinted, then the female cop took her to a room where she watched her remove her clothing, including her undergarments.

After Catalina pulled on a baggy orange jumpsuit, the cop took her to a restroom where the stalls had no doors.

The woman handed her a urine sample cup. "You've never been arrested before, have you?"

Catalina shook her head as she took the cup.

"I'm sorry, but I have to watch your every movement."

Catalina dropped her jumpsuit and sat on the commode.

"Believe it or not, just last week I brought a woman in here, and she had a syringe, primed and ready, hidden in her..." She nodded toward Catalina's lap.

"Good God." Catalina screwed the cap on the urine sample and put the warm container in the cop's gloved hand.

"When people get hooked on that crap, they'll do just about anything."

Catalina pulled up the jumpsuit. "Now what?"

"I'll take you to a holding cell while the lab works on this sample. You wanta wash your hands?"

Catalina nodded.

She was placed in a holding cell with a dozen other women, where metal benches were bolted to three of the walls.

She glanced around. Most of the women looked like hookers. Two of them seemed very agitated, repeatedly rubbing their arms and thighs, standing to pace before the bars, then sitting for a moment before starting the rubbing and pacing again. The women ranged in age from college girls to grandmothers. All of them smelled like homeless bums from the street. Maybe they were.

Catalina wanted to sit, close her eyes, and shut out everything. But without a can of Lysol or Clorox wipes, there was no way she was going to sit on those benches. So, she stood in a corner, leaning against the bars, as far away from the others as she could get.

* * * * *

Several hours passed before a female cop, a different one, came to get Catalina. She cuffed her and took her to a small room where a metal table was bolted to the floor.

The cop linked her cuffs to a bracket in the table and locked it.

"Sit," the cop said, then left, banging the door closed.

Is this worth going to prison? If I tell them the truth, it might get me off the hook, but that only puts someone else in here. If I had a slick lawyer...

The detective in gray came in, dropped some papers on the table, then sat and slowly went through them.

Intimidation. Control. What's next, 'Can't we be friends?'

"I'm Detective William Beals. You're charged with possession of a controlled substance, with intent to distribute." He looked at her, waiting.

She stared at him.

"We had Willie Dublin under surveillance when you met him at Forty-seventh and Washington, slipped five hundred to him..." He opened a large brown envelope and dumped out five Benjamins. "These exact bills. Then he gave you three grams of heroin and three syringes wrapped in a red scarf." He opened another envelope and poured out the contents. "These drugs, the syringes, and this red scarf. Right?"

"You said I have the right to remain silent."

"Oh, God. All I'm trying to do is establish the facts. You're not on trial yet."

"You also said anything I say, can and will be used against me in a court of law."

"I said that because I have to say it. I repeat it a hundred times a week. It doesn't mean shit."

"It means anything I say, can and will be used against me in a court of law."

"You watch too much TV. All I'm trying to do is lay out the events you were involved in this morning. Is that so difficult?"

Catalina's cuffs rattled when she leaned down to scratch her nose. She remained silent.

"Shit." He stood. "You can sit here and rot for the rest of the day for all I care." He left everything on the table and went out, banging the door closed.

Catalina glanced at the large mirror on the wall. She looked closer, then leaned down to her hands to straighten a stray lock of hair. Looking in the mirror again, she turned her head to the side, then the other side, as if admiring her appearance.

She was dying to look through the stuff he left on the table, but she knew he—and probably a few other cops—were watching her through the mirrored glass.

They want me to look through the papers and paraphernalia. Why? Fingerprints?

She leaned back and yawned. After a moment, she closed her eyes.

Catalina didn't have a watch, but she knew it had

been over an hour since Detective Beals had left the room.

A woman in a trim business suit came in. "Hi. I'm Mary Grant."

"Ah, the good cop."

Mary laughed. "I try to be. I see the bad cop has already been here." Catalina nodded.

"Did he explain everything?" Her only adornment was a mother-of-pearl broach pinned above her left breast. It contrasted nicely with the navy blue material of her skirt-suit.

Catalina stared at the broach. *Sweet.* She nodded her response to the woman's question.

"Is there anything you want to ask me?"

Catalina shrugged.

"So, here's where we are. You had no evidence of drugs in your system, no needle tracks, and you don't display the typical characteristics of a drug addict."

Catalina smiled.

"Do you want to go through any of this stuff?"

She shook her head.

"God, how I hate Miranda."

Catalina laughed. "Oops, can that be used against me?"

"Sure, I can take laughter to the judge. He'll probably laugh, too, just after he gives you a year in the joint."

Catalina waited.

"That's the guidelines since this is your first offense and you're not a user."

"Is that a family heirloom?" Catalina asked.

"What?"

"Your broach."

"Oh." Mary looked down and touched it. "No. I bought it for myself, last Christmas. Got it from Amazon."

"Can I look at it?"

"I guess so." She unpinned it and handed it to Catalina, who ran a fingertip around the edge.

So smooth.

She examined the back, then laid it on the table.

A perfect oval.

"Shouldn't my lawyer be in here?" she asked.

"Do you have one?"

"No."

"Can you afford one?"

"No."

"At your hearing, the judge will appoint a public defender for you."

"When will that happen?"

"Anywhere from six to eight weeks."

"Crap."

"Can you make bail?"

"How much is that?"

"Five thousand."

"Shit, I couldn't make five hundred bail. That's all I had." She nodded to the five one-hundred-dollar bills on the table.

"In that case, you'll be a guest of New York City for the next six to eight weeks."

"Wonderful."

"What were you doing, trying to become a dealer?"

"I paid retail for that crap. How could I make a profit?"

"What, then?"

"I'm doing research for a book. I wanted to see what it was like to get high."

"You could do that on one hit. You bought enough for three fixes."

"I didn't know how much it would take to get high."

"You would've ODed and died if you shot up all that at once."

"Well, I guess it's a good thing your guys showed up when you did."

Mary began gathering the papers and evidence.

Catalina clasped her hands on the table before herself.

"All right. We'll wait to see what the judge thinks of your story."

* * * * *

Catalina was uncuffed, given a tin cup, and placed in a cell with a middle-aged woman who looked like a schoolteacher. She was asleep on the bottom bunk.

Sheets, a blanket, and a pillow were stacked on the top bunk.

Catalina made the bed, trying not to disturb the woman. She climbed onto the bunk and lay back, staring at the ceiling.

I'm a drug dealer, in jail for maybe a year, and I've lost my place at Qubit's Incubator. How much worse could it be?

She felt for something in the side pocket of her jumpsuit. Smiling, she held up the policewoman's mother-of-pearl broach to catch the light.

Ovals never lie.

* * * * *

The sound of the toilet flushing woke Catalina late in the afternoon.

"Lidar!" She sat up on her bunk, rubbing her eyes.

"Sorry, Luv," her cellmate said. "What's that you said?"

"Um, nothing. It was just a crazy dream."

The woman washed her hands in the stainless steel sink, then glanced in the shiny metal mirror bolted to the wall. She straightened her gray hair.

Catalina swung her legs over the edge of the bunk.

"Almost feeding time," the woman said.

"Great. I haven't had anything since breakfast."

"Good thing. That'll make the beans and weenies look delicious. I'm Madeline Cartwright."

"Catalina Saylor. What're you in for?"

"Murder. They think I killed my husband."

"Did you?"

"Yeah. The bastard cheated on me. The other woman's a granny, older than me."

"Justifiable homicide."

"I agree. What they got on you?"

"Dealing drugs."

"What did your lawyer say?"

"Don't have one. What do you do for a living?"

"I teach Braille reading."

"Really?" Catalina said. "It must be hard to learn to read by feeling those grooves cut into paper."

"It just takes practice. You'd be surprised how fast a blind person learns to feel those lines and curves. How'd you get into dealing drugs?"

If she's a Braille teacher, I'm a sumo wrestler.

"My mom showed me the ropes before she ODed."

Two metal trays scraped on the cement floor as they were shoved through a slot at the bottom of the cell door.

"How'd you hook up with your drug dealer?"

Madeline asked.

"Google." Catalina took a bite of her pork-and-beans. "This's not bad."

"I guess you are starving."

They sat together on Madeline's bunk.

"What'd your lawyer tell you?" Catalina asked.

"He wants me to plead manslaughter. But I'm holding out for innocence on the grounds of temporary insanity."

"That might work."

"How many dopers you selling to?"

Wow, Madeline. Really subtle. "About twenty." *I'll give her so much bullshit, Detective Beals will know I'm onto him.*

"How do you deal with so many? By text?"

"No, nothing electronic or in writing. We use trash signals."

"How's that work?" Madeline took a bite.

"Candy wrappers. If Junkie 'A' wants a gram, he leaves an Almond Joy wrapper under a rock beside a trash bin at the corner of Forty-Seventh and Ninth Avenue. When I have his drop ready, I put the Almond Joy wrapper on the other side of the bin. He leaves his money behind a loose brick in the alley off Ninth Avenue, between West Twentieth and West Twenty-first streets. I pick up the money and leave his happy powder behind the brick. Junkie 'B' uses a Hershey wrapper, and so on."

"Clever. You must do a pretty good business."

Catalina chewed a bite. "Yeah, about forty grand a month, take home." *That'll give Beals enough for him to find a new snitch.*

"Hey, Saylor." Keys jangled against the bars when a guard opened the door. "You got a visitor."

* * * * *

"Holy crap!" Catalina took the chair across from her visitor in the common room. "You're the last person I expected to see."

"There's only two of us," Morticadi said. "We have to stick together." She pushed a red box across the table.

Catalina lifted the lid from the little box and caught her breath.

"Here's the wrapping paper and bow." Morticadi laid the black paper covered with grinning silver skulls on the gray plastic table. "The Gestapo made me open it outside to be sure it wasn't a bomb or a donut."

Catalina took the object from the box, holding it to the light.

The pale, honey-colored stone was a spherical oval in a rounded egg shape. It could have been a polished orb of amber containing an ancient butterfly, but instead it held something much more interesting.

"You brought me a weapon!"

A huge female guard jerked her head toward them.

Catalina held up the oval for the guard to see.

The guard huffed and turned her attention to a lemon-meringue pie at another table being sliced with a white plastic knife.

"You brought me a weapon!" Catalina whispered.

Morticadi grinned.

Inside the golden Lucite, a tiny AK-47 floated in chilling detail.

"This looks expensive."

"Yes, it would've been."

Catalina turned it, feeling the velvety smooth surface. "Where did you, um, borrow it?"

"Bloomingdale's, on Broadway. They were having a sale."

"Yeah, right. They just didn't know it. I love this. If you ever get locked up, I'll bring you something. How's your dad doing with his project?"

"He said he's done the first crispr edit and he's waiting to see the results. Can you teach me CGI coding?"

"Sure. As soon as I get out of here, we'll get started. Of course, that might be five years from now."

"No. You find a slick shyster lawyer, and she'll get you off."

"I wish I had a lawyer, even a shyster one. Anyway, in the meantime, go to my website, and you'll find some ten-second clips, along with the source code for each one. Have you had any computer programming in school?"

"Yes, Java script."

"Good. Python is a little different. Look at the code for the jumping cricket, then watch the tutorial video. Next time you come to visit, bring your iPad, and I'll get you started on coding."

"What's your website, jailbird-dot-com?"

Catalina laughed. "Close. Try catalinasaylor-dot-com."

"How clever to disguise the name like that."

"Yeah." She caressed the oval, feeling the perfect natality, the almost soft surface. "When I get sprung, we're going shoplifting together."

* * * * *

Around mid-morning of the next day, a female guard came to the cell.

"Saylor, you been sprung."

"Really?" Catalina climbed down from her bunk

95

and slipped into her flip-flops. "How'd that happen?"

The guard swung open the door. "Proly somebody paid your bail."

"Should I take my cup?"

"Nah, leave it."

A trustee handed over her clothing and phone. No one watched her get dressed.

The guard walked her to the front desk.

Catalina stopped, staring at the man waiting for her. "What the hell, McGill?"

Chapter Nine

McGill shrugged. His smile softened his usual scowl.

"You're the last person I expected to see," Catalina said.

"Hey, Saylor," the officer behind the glass said. "You want your stuff or not?"

She stared at McGill for another moment, then turned to the officer.

"Your purse, cell phone, one tiny screwdriver, and a name plate. Sign here."

Catalina signed the form fastened to a clipboard. "Thanks."

"Have a good one," the officer said.

She checked her messages; there were fourteen.

'I just got out of jail,' she texted Marilyn. 'You'll never believe who bailed me out.'

The next reply went to Morticadi. 'I'm free!'

"You hungry?" McGill asked.

"Yeah, I missed my breakfast of beans and weenies. What's in the box?"

"Stuff from your desk."

"Ah, yeah." She took the box; it wasn't heavy. "I wondered how my time in the Incubator would end."

"You'd still be there if you hadn't foolishly helped other people."

He held open the door for her to leave the police

station ahead of him.

"I actually don't think I could've solved the human-computer interface in six months, let alone thirty days," she said as she tossed her box in the back seat of his Camry.

"How about pancakes?" he asked.

"Yes! And coffee."

* * * * *

At the local IHOP, McGill took a bite of a dripping pancake. "When's your court hearing?"

"Fifteenth of next month." Catalina pinned the oval broach on her chest, then unpinned it to reposition it.

"You have a lawyer?"

"I guess the judge will assign a public defender to me." Catalina sipped her coffee.

"You might as well represent yourself. What's your defense?"

"They found drugs and paraphernalia in my desk. I have no defense."

"Someone planted them?"

"No."

They ate in silence for a while.

McGill picked up his napkin. "I know you don't do drugs, and you don't deal. So, the only explanation is that you bought the stuff for someone else."

"That's my defense?"

"I don't know. What else can you do? I hate to see you locked up."

She narrowed her eyes on him, then added more butter to the top of her waffles. "How's Joe doing?"

"He got a cubicle, thanks to you."

"Good   for   him."

"You know who's a lawyer?"

She looked at McGill as she chewed.

"Ponicar."

"Monarch Ponicar?"

He nodded.

"He received a patent on his therapeutic water body," she said.

"Yes. Before coming to the Incubator, he practiced law."

"Do you know what happened to my moped?" Catalina asked. "It was in the parking lot when I was arrested."

"Yeah. I took it inside. It's in the supply room."

* * * * *

The next afternoon, Catalina picked up her tip from beside the remains of spaghetti and meatballs. She slipped the five into her apron pocket.

"Order up."

Hugo slid a plate onto the shelf separating the kitchen from the counter area. The meal was a rare T-bone steak, with mashed potatoes and brown gravy.

"Got it," Catalina said. "Hey, Hugo. That old maid said her salad was limp."

"Gretchen?"

"Yeah."

"Was she smiling?"

"Uh-huh."

On her way to deliver the T-bone, her phone vibrated against her thigh. She placed the platter of meat and potatoes before a slim guy in an O.D. green uniform. 'New York City Sanitation Department' was emblazoned on his shoulder patch.

"Can I sweeten your coffee, Cal?"

"Oh, yeah." Cal grinned as he picked up his knife and fork.

After delivering a fresh cup of coffee to Cal, Catalina checked her message.

'Hey, Cat. I need a tiny hydraulic valve.' It was a text from old Edison.

'How tiny?'

'Less than two millimeters.'

'That's micro tiny. Did you try printing one?'

'Yeah. All I got was a dime-sized lump of gray plastic.'

'You got a detailed sketch?'

'Yes.'

'Text it to me, Edison. I have to work till eleven tonight, but I'll take a look at it when I get home. Also I'll need your ID and password to get into the Qubit server.'

'You got it, pal.'

* * * * *

Late the next morning, Catalina pulled her pink, frilly dress over her head and began brushing her hair, getting ready to go take care of the lunch hour rush at the café. She slipped her screwdriver and nameplate into her pocket.

Her phone vibrated. She picked it up from beside the bathroom sink.

'A thing of beauty is a joy forever.'

She smiled; it was from Edison.

'Yeah, but did it work?'

She reached to straighten the oval picture on her wall. It contained a series of hieroglyphs chiseled into stone.

'Perfectly. I got coolant flowing end to end. When you coming back to the bullpen?'

'Five to ten, Edison. Gotta run.'

'KK. I'll bake you a cake.'

* * * * *

At mid-afternoon, when the rush had calmed down to a lazy afternoon of a few stockbrokers pretending to discuss business with heavily made-up young women, Catalina took her break to sit with a guy from Qubit's Incubator.

"Monarch Ponicar," she said as she slipped into the booth across from him. She set her Coke on the table. "Thanks for coming to see me."

He reached to take her offered hand. "Call me 'Mike,' and I haven't been in a courtroom in over five years."

"That's okay. I'm not asking you to take on my case. I just need basic advice."

"When I was a trial lawyer, it was mostly contract disputes. I never handled criminal cases."

"I don't have any money to pay you, but if you can just put me on the right track, I'll figure it out from there."

"You won't owe me anything, because I know about the people you've helped at the Incubator. The least I can do is offer you a little advice."

"Even if I don't hire you, you'll be bound by attorney-client privilege, right?"

He nodded.

"I bought those drugs for a friend. He was broke, coming up against his thirty-day make-or-break date, and his supplier was about to blow his knees away with a thirty-eight. I know it was a stupid thing to do, but he's basically a good guy who got caught up in something bigger than himself.”

“You’re talking about Adu Dhabi Wilson.”

“Yes, otherwise known as ‘Joe.’”

“That’s what I thought.”

“How’s he doing?” she asked.

“He got a cubicle.”

“I know. McGill told me. But how’s he doing?”

“As far as I know, okay. But a junkie is always going to be a junkie until he ODs or gets locked up.”

“If I tell the judge I was buying for a friend, but not give his name, will it go badly for me?”

“What do the cops have on you?”

She told him about the three grams of heroin and syringes found in her desk and that they had the dealer under surveillance when she made the buy.

“They charged me with possession, with the intent to distribute.”

“Well, that’s enough to get you one-to-five. You have any priors? Drugs, speeding, theft...”

Catalina sipped her Coke, then felt in her dress pocket for something.

“Don’t tell me you’ve got a criminal record?”

She laid her oval nameplate on the table and pushed it to him.

“Evangeline Psychiatric Hospital,” he read the inscription aloud.

“I’m a kleptomaniac.”

“That got you put away in a psychiatric hospital?”

“I had a choice of that or jail time. After six months at Evangeline, they said I was cured, and the court expunged my records.”

“You have documentation?” Mike asked.

“Yes.”

"Were you cured?"

"I stole that nameplate on the day I left Evangeline."

Mike laughed. "Are you still stealing?"

She nodded. "I have to. I see an oval-shaped object, and everything else melts from my view. I stole this broach from the female detective who questioned me."

Mike stared at the broach pinned to her uniform. "How did you...never mind. Why don't you just buy oval things?"

"I tried that, but it was meaningless. I have to take it. An oval is no good to me unless it belonged to somebody. I stole an earring from Tracy."

"Tracy? As in Victor's assistant at the Incubator?"

"Yes, and I took that oval picture from behind his desk."

"I noticed that was gone."

"It's hanging on my bathroom wall. So, without a criminal record, but not implicating the guy I was buying for, what are my chances?"

Mike sipped his cold coffee, then stared out the window for a moment. "Two possible outcomes. The judge will either give you a year in jail or a hundred hours of community service."

"How do I get the commserv?" Catalina asked.

"Bring four or five character witnesses to the trial."

"Marilyn, my roomie, might speak up for me, and maybe Hugo." She nodded toward the kitchen. "He's my boss. But I don't know of anyone else."

"I know of at least eight more, counting me."

"I never did anything for you."

"No," Mike said, "but I know what you did for Joe, Edison, Lew, and the others."

“But would they take the stand?”

“No doubt.”

Catalina sipped her Coke. She took a deep breath and slowly let it out.

“You want me to be a character witness, or…” Mike hesitated.

“Or what?”

“Argue your case before the judge?”

She smiled. “You said you don’t do courtrooms anymore.”

“I’ll come out of retirement for this one.” He held Catalina’s steady gaze for a moment. “There may a third possibility.”

“What’s that?”

“Ask the judge to dismiss the charges at the hearing.”

“On what grounds?”

“I’ll try to come up with an approach to do an end run around the prosecutor.”

“I can’t pay you until I sell my echolocation gadget.”

“The Romans had a term for a situation such as this. Perhaps you’ve heard of it; *pro bona*.”

“You want a fresh cup of coffee, Mike?”

* * * * *

At six the next evening, Catalina received a text from Alex; ‘Joe ODed in his cubicle.’

‘Oh, no,’ she texted. ‘Is he okay?’

‘We called 911. The medics took him to the hospital. They left about five minutes ago.’

‘Which hospital?’

‘Mount Sinai West.’

'Thx.'

Catalina told her boss she had to go to the hospital and ran out to flag down a taxi.

Ten minutes later she stood at the hospital's admitting desk. The nurse could only tell Catalina that Joe was still in the ER and alive. Any information beyond that could only be given to a relative.

"I don't even know if he has any relatives in New York," Catalina said.

"All you can do is wait, honey," the nurse said. "I'll let you know what happens."

Catalina clicked out a message to Morticadi while she waited.

A half hour later, Edison and Tafi Ari Rivo hurried in.

"Any news?" Edison asked.

Catalina shook her head. "All I know is, he was still alive ten minutes ago."

They sat in the chairs on either side of her.

"He must've been shooting up right there in his cubicle," Ari said.

"Why can't he just leave that crap alone?" Catalina asked.

"I think it's the crap that won't leave him alone," old man Edison said.

Morticadi came in to wait with Catalina. She glanced at Catalina's uniform. "I like your broach."

Catalina squeezed her hand.

* * * * *

The next day, Catalina had the second shift at the café. During an afternoon lull, she sat at the counter and checked her messages.

'Help!' It was from pissant Mickey Houser.

'What up, Mic?'

'I need a rotating bracket for my laser weed-eater.'

'3-D printer.'

'Yeah, right.'

'Did you try it?" Catalina texted.

'I got a square bracket and a half gear with no teeth. Everyone says you're the 3-D printer expert.'

She smiled. 'I'm not there anymore, Mic.'

'So? Old Edison said you did a valve for him last week without even coming into the Incubator."

'Do you have all your other parts?'

'Urm. I made a handle from a broomstick.'

'Do you have the parts drawn out to scale?'

'Yes.'

'I don't get off shift till 11. Before you leave, load 1.75 mm metal-filled filament in the printer and leave it on.'

'k.'

'Meet me at 10 west 15th street, apartment 324.'

'Got it.'

'Bring adult beverage.'

'Ok, metal filament, adult beverage, apartment 324. C U at 11:30.'

* * * * *

Catalina and Mickey didn't finish programming the 3-D printer until almost 7 a.m. She had the second shift so she didn't bother trying to get any sleep.

In the café's kitchen, she helped the dishwasher guy catch up on the pots and pans.

Her phone rang in the middle of the afternoon. She answered using her Bluetooth earbud.

"Victor and Tracy just came in for demos," Tafi said.

"Who's up?"

"Mickey and his laser weed-eater."

"Cool," Catalina said. "Can you stream it?"

"Sure."

She hung up and dried her hands as she walked toward the grill. "Hey, Hugo. You gotta see this."

"What is it?" Hugo asked as he cleaned the grill with a Brillo pad.

"One of the guys at the Incubator is going to do a presentation."

Her phone chimed, and when she answered, Tafi told her the livestream was ready to roll. She then set up her iPad on the counter, and Hugo, the other waitress, and two customers watched the screen with her.

Mickey stepped onto the stage, carrying a large crate. Edison followed, with a second crate. Mickey set his box on the stage, then took out squares of turf with tall grass and weeds. He arranged the turf into a lawn-like area measuring about six feet by eight feet.

After going back to his desk, he returned with his weed-eater and plugged it into a wall outlet.

"Later on," Mickey said, "it'll have optional solar power using Drover's solar-cell jacket."

Tafi stepped around to the side of the stage get a better view when Mickey was ready to begin.

Mickey clicked on the weed-eater, and a red laser beam shot from the oscillating head. The tiny beam of light sliced through the weeds and grass like a razor-sharp scythe, producing a perfectly trimmed lawn.

"That looks really dangerous," someone said from behind Tafi.

"Of course McGill would have a complaint,"

Catalina whispered.

"The metal shield," Mickey said, "is ten inches in front of the laser head. It prevents the beam from going farther than that."

"What if you trip over something?" one of the pissants asked. "And you fall with your hand landing in the laser beam?"

"It has two pressure switches." Mickey removed his left hand from the shaft of the weed-eater, and the laser beam instantly died. "The switches are located eight inches apart, and both must be pressed down for the machine to operate."

"Someone could put duct tape over one of them," McGill said.

"Yes, if he was determined to bypass the safety feature. But the same could be done with a conventional string weed-eater. Then the idiot could put his hand into the string area and slice off his fingers."

Someone laughed.

"How much does that thing cost?" Hugo asked. "Look how perfect the grass is cut. I could really use that, and when it has solar power, so much the better."

"It's just a prototype, Hugo," Catalina said. "Not for sale yet."

"Well, sign me up on the waiting list."

Catalina picked up her phone. "Tafi, tell Mickey he has five people here at Hugo's Café watching his demo and Hugo wants to be first on his waiting list to buy the weed-eater."

"Make that two people," one of the café customers said.

"Three," the other one said.

Tafi relayed the message, and several people in the Incubator shouted that they wanted to be on the waiting list, too.

Mickey grinned and glanced at Victor.

After a whispered conversation with Tracy, Victor said, "Cubicle twelve."

"Yes!" Mickey said, then turned toward Tafi's phone and gave Catalina a thumbs-up.

* * * * *

Catalina's hearing began at 1 in the afternoon in courtroom number 4 at the New York County Courthouse, 60 Centre Street, in Manhattan.

She sat alone at the defendant's table, wearing her orange jumpsuit—apparently, the jailers had already decided the outcome of her hearing.

The back door squeaked open, and she turned to watch the Assistant DA come in, followed by two lawyers who looked like adolescent surfers. All three stared at Catalina, then the DA smiled. They took the plaintiff's table, with the two lawyer-kids sitting to the DA's right. All three were dressed in charcoal gray suits and wore matching red ties.

The back door opened again, and an elderly man limped in. He was followed by a tall young man in a navy-blue suit, wearing a chauffer's cap. He helped the old man sit on the bench at the back of the gallery, then sat beside him and removed his cap.

Judge Solomon Phillips came in, and after everyone stood, he waved them to sit down. The old man hadn't quite gotten to his feet when his chauffer helped him back down.

The back door opened and two more people came in.

The judge took his seat in a high-backed

executive's chair behind the bench. "Let's get started, Mr. Siskit."

"Yes, sir." Assistant District Attorney Benjamin Siskit stood, and his two lawyers jumped to their feet. He whispered something, and they dropped back to their chairs. "Your Honor, the State of New York plans to charge Miss Catalina Saylor with purchasing illegal drugs, with intent to sell."

"Are you prepared to show probable cause?"

"Yes, sir." Mr. Siskit sat.

"Miss Saylor," the judge said, "it appears you're representing yourself."

She glanced at the three people at the other table.

Mr. Siskit grinned like a happy coyote.

"No, Your Honor."

She turned to look toward the spectators; there were five people. Morticadi smiled from where she sat directly behind Catalina. She reached to pat Catalina's shoulder.

One of the others stood. "Attorney Michael Ponicar, Your Honor," he said.

"I've never seen you in my courtroom before."

"No, sir. I haven't tried a case in over five years."

"Are your credentials up to date?"

"I entered my information online last night."

The judge glanced at his clerk, who was already typing on her keyboard.

"How you spelling that last name?" she asked.

Mike spelled it for her.

After a moment, the clerk looked at the judge. "All in order, Your Honor. His last case was five years, three months ago. It was a real estate contract dispute. His client lost."

"Mr. Siskit," the judge said. "Do you have any

objection to Mr. Ponicar trying this case?"

Mr. Siskit stood. "No, sir." His grin grew even wider than before.

"All right. Let the records show Mr. Ponicar has been examined and accepted. You may join your client."

Catalina reached to shake hands with Mike when he pushed the gate open and went to her table.

"Shall we begin, Mr. Siskit?" the judge said.

The back door opened, and two people came in. Lucius Pritchard and his wife Katrina hurried down the aisle and sat beside Morticadi. They smiled a greeting to Catalina.

The judge cleared his throat. "Mr. Siskit..."

The door opened again. Tafi Ari Rivo and Tim Alexander entered the room.

Catalina glanced at the judge, then watched them take seats in the back of the courtroom. Tafi waved to Catalina.

Before the judge could say anything, old Edison came in. He gave Catalina a thumbs-up and sat beside Tafi.

The judge stared at the smiling Edison for a moment. "Deputy Applegate," he said. "Go take a look in the corridor," he pointed his gavel toward the back door, "and see if there are any more spectators about to interrupt these proceedings."

"Yes, sir." The female deputy went to the door and, holding it open, said, "You people looking for the Catalina Saylor hearing?"

She stepped inside, holding open the door.

McGill came in, followed by Roger Collingsworth, Journey Covey, and Alex Drover. They took seats in front of Edison.

As Catalina watched, William Clarkson, a monarch, came in with two others she'd only met in passing at the Incubator.

Marilyn, her roommate, along with three of her friends came in.

Behind them were two more; Victor Templeton and Tracy. They, along with all the others, sat on Catalina's side of the courtroom.

"Is that it, Sylvia?" the judge asked.

Deputy Sylvia Applegate stepped out and glanced down the hall. "Yes, sir."

"If anyone else tries to come in, tell them this courtroom is closed."

Catalina was almost in tears as she watched the smiling faces of all the people who came to support her.

She was jolted by the judge banging his gavel.

"Once again," the judge, "Mr. Siskit, shall we begin?"

"Yes, sir. The Prosecution calls Madeline Cartwright."

The woman who'd shared Catalina's jail cell came forward, was sworn in, and took her seat in the witness box.

Siskit asked her if she knew the defendant.

"Yes, sir. I met her in the city jail."

He asked her to recount their conversations in the jail cell.

After her testimony, the judge waved Mike forward.

"Madeline Cartwright," Mike said as he approached the witness stand.

"Yes, sir."

"You shared a cell with Catalina Saylor, it that correct?"

"Yes."

"Why were you in jail?"

“Assault.”

“Did this assault result in death?”

“Um…no.”

“What is your occupation, Miss Cartwright?” Mike asked.

“I’m a paralegal.”

“Oh.” Mike flipped a page of the papers he held. “It says here you’re a teacher of Braille.”

“Yes. I teach it to the blind.”

“Hmm…” He read something else on his clipboard. “I have no further questions at this time, Your Honor, but I reserve the right to recall Miss Cartwright.”

“Fine,” the judge said. “Go take a seat in the gallery, Miss Cartwright, and wait there.”

“The Defense calls Detective William Beals.”

After Beals was sworn in and took a seat in the witness box, Mike questioned him.

“Detective, you received information from Catalina Saylor’s cellmate to the effect that Miss Saylor ran a profitable business of selling illegal and controlled substances. Is that correct?”

“Yes, sir.”

“In Miss Cartwright’s testimony in this Court, she said Miss Saylor conducted her drug business by receiving payment and dispensing drugs using a loose brick in the alley off Ninth Avenue, between West Twentieth and West Twenty-first streets. It that an accurate statement?”

“Yes.”

“Did you or any of your associates go to that alley and find the loose brick and order the CSI department to conduct lab work to detect traces of illegal drugs?”

“Uh…no.”

“Why is that?”

“We found no loose bricks in that alley.”

"But you did observe people who appeared to be drug users placing candy wrappers beneath a rock beside a trash bin at the corner of Forty-Seventh and Ninth Avenue?"

"We had the trash bin under surveillance for three days, but no one left candy wrappers under a rock."

"I have no further questions for this witness, Your Honor, but I would like to now recall Miss Madeline Cartwright to the stand."

After Miss Cartwright was reminded of her oath and took her seat, Mike stood before her for a moment, watching her fidget.

He took a thick sheet of paper from a manila folder. "Miss Cartwright, would you please read this to the Court?"

She took the sheet of paper, glanced at it, then turned it over. "Read what?"

"The words, Miss Cartwright," Mike said. "Please read the words."

"There's no words here to read," she said.

"If you look closely, you will see the page is filled with a series of raised dots. There are three hundred words on that piece of paper, written in Braille."

"Oh, yes. I see that now."

"And since you are a teacher of Braille to the blind, I would ask that you use your fingertips to interpret those dots and read the words to the Court."

"Well...I...I've not actually progressed far enough in my training to actually read Braille."

"But you told Miss Saylor you were a teacher of Braille, and you also testified under oath in this courtroom that you are a teacher of Braille, correct?"

"I meant to say I wanted to be a teacher of Braille."

Mike took the paper from Madeline and handed it to the judge. "Your Honor, I would like to enter this page of Braille into evidence."

The judge took the paper and ran his fingertips over the raised dots.

"I would also respectfully request," Mike said, "that all of Miss Cartwright's testimony be stricken from the record. It's obviously a total fabrication."

"So ordered." Judge Phillips handed the paper to the bailiff. "Mark this as exhibit 'B,' Herman." The judge turned to Madeline. "Since you say you're a paralegal, Miss Cartwright, I'm sure you're aware that you've perjured yourself in my courtroom. Now, if you'll please step down and go to that very pleasant lady standing just there," he pointed to a woman dressed in a New York City Jail uniform, "she'll escort you to your new temporary quarters." He turned back toward Mike. "Would you like to call any other witnesses, Counselor?"

"Yes, sir. The Defense calls Miss Catalina Saylor to the stand."

Catalina was duly sworn in and took her seat in the witness box.

"Did you intend to sell the drugs you purchased from Willie Dublin?" Mike asked.

"No, sir."

"Were you going to use those drugs yourself?"

"No, sir."

"What, then, were you planning to do with them?"

"Donate them to a friend who was in dire need."

"What's his name?"

"I'd rather not answer that." Catalina glanced at the scowling judge.

"Why?" Mike asked.

"I don't want to get him into any more trouble

than he's already in."

"If it pleases the Court," Mike said to the judge, "the defense would like to excuse Miss Saylor so that we might call another wittiness."

"You're excused, Miss Saylor," the judge said. "Who is your next witness?"

"We have a video link to the Hazelden Betty Ford Foundation, at Two-Eighty-Three W. Broadway, here in the city."

"What is that place?" the judge asked.

"It's a drug rehab center," Mike said.

"All right. Put it on the big screen."

Mike nodded to the computer tech, and soon the video link was established and an image came on the screen.

Catalina caught her breath when she saw the person on the screen.

"Your name, please," Mike said.

"Adu Dhabi Wilson."

"I believe most people call you 'Joe,' is that correct?"

"Yes, sir."

Joe was sworn in by the bailiff.

"Did Catalina Saylor sell or offer to sell illegal drugs to you?" Mike asked.

"No, she did not."

"Do you know she is on trial for purchasing illegal drugs, with intent to sell?"

"Yes. When I told her about my habit and how I owed my dealer over forty thousand dollars and he was threatening to kneecap me, she offered to buy the heroin and give it to me."

"Give it to you? Not sell it to you?"

"That's right. I was under a great deal of pressure

to finish my project at Qubit's Incubator, and she knew I couldn't handle the pressure without two or three fixes a day. After she was arrested, I found a street dealer, got five grams on credit, then, like an idiot, I ODed on that crap. I was taken to the hospital, where I almost died. Now I'm lucky to be here at the Betty Ford Rehab Center."

"Catalina Saylor never asked you for money for the heroin?" Mike asked.

"No, she was going to give me one hit at a time to keep me going. Catalina stopped working on her own project to help me, along with helping several others at the Incubator. She has a heart of gold, and when I get out of here in six months, I'm going to do everything I can to help her. It would be a sin to put a good person like her in jail."

Mike glanced at the judge, who nodded. Mike then thanked Joe for his testimony.

"Will the defendant please stand," the judge said.

When Mike was back at her table, they waited to see what the judge would do.

"Mr. Siskit," the judge said to the prosecutor. "This may be the flimsiest case you've ever brought before this court. I suggest the next time you use a jailhouse snitch, you put a wire on her, and then double check your facts before charging someone with a crime."

"Yes, sir," Mr. Siskit said.

"You'll now drop any and all charges against Miss Catalina Saylor. This case is closed. Miss Saylor, you are free—"

The cheers and applause drowned him out.

Judge Phillips let it go on for a few moments before pounding his gavel to regain control of his courtroom.

"Miss Saylor, you are free to go," he said, then stood and left the bench.

Catalina threw her arms around Mike's neck and kissed his cheek. "Brilliant! You were absolutely brilliant."

He hugged her back. "Well, once we blew Madeline Cartwright's testimony out of the water, it was pretty much all over."

She leaned back away from Mike. "Can I buy you a drink?"

"You can buy me a lot of drinks."

She looked around at all the people crowding the railing, waiting to congratulate her.

"In fact," she grinned at McGill, "if I can borrow some money, I'm buying

beer for everyone, and pizza."

That brought another round of cheers.

"Except you, Goth Girl." She put her arm around Morticadi's shoulders. "You get nothing but a Coke."

"That's okay." The girl held Catalina's hand. "But I get your jumpsuit, right?"

Chapter Ten

Two months after the trail, Catalina sat in front of Victor's desk.

"You're the first person ever to be asked to return to Qubit's Incubator." Victor smiled at Catalina.

"Thank you, Mr. Templeton," Catalina said. "I'm so grateful." She glanced at Tracy, sitting beside her. *Is that a smile? Another first.*

"Now," Victor said, "let's see if you can earn yourself a cubicle in the next thirty days. I can almost guarantee you won't be asked back a second time."

"Can I have a dorm room?"

Tracy slapped her hand over her mouth.

"Seriously?" Victor said. "I give you the first ever second chance, and you have the balls to ask for a favor?"

Catalina nodded.

"Room twelve is vacant," Tracy said.

Victor laughed. "Go move your crap into room twelve, and get out of my office before you ask for room service."

* * * * *

That afternoon, Catalina slapped a sticky note on

Joe's computer screen.

He had only been back for a few days, but already had his patent application ready to send in.

He stopped typing and whispered, "Midnight, room twelve, bring adult beverage."

She pressed a second note to the back of Tafi's hand as she worked on her germ visualization project.

"Midnight, room twelve. Bring chips." Tafi laughed. "Be there."

Catalina gave similar notes to McGill, Lew, and Tim.

At midnight, Qubit's Incubator was empty, except for dorm room twelve, where music, laughter, and the clinking of glasses could be heard for many hours.

Chapter Eleven

Twenty-three days after Catalina returned to Qubit's Incubator, Victor came into the bullpen, and Catalina was first to be called to the stage.

As she donned her gear, Tracy held open the door for the old man she'd seen in the back row of the courtroom. As he limped to a chair beside Victor, the same young man in the navy-blue suit and chauffer's cap followed him. He helped the old man sit, then stood behind him and removed his hat.

Catalina walked toward the stage with a first baseman's glove on her left hand and red bandana tied across her eyes. Two tiny blue wires ran from the cap to a power supply in her Hello Kitty backpack.

As she neared the stage, she held out her right hand as one might feel for a table in a dark room. When she was just inches away from the stage, she lifted her right foot onto the edge and stepped up.

She then faced the others in the bullpen, adjusted her blue baseball cap, and waited.

"What's she doing?" someone whispered.

Catalina pressed a finger to her lips.

Joe shouted from the far right side of the room. She spun around, with her right hand extended in that direction. She then stretched up high to her left, but the baseball he threw grazed the web of her glove and flew away.

"Here comes another one," Joe said.

She knelt and scooped up the ball as it flew toward her just an inch off the floor.

Several people cheered and clapped.

"One more," Joe yelled as he threw another ball up toward the rafters, seventy-five feet above.

Catalina dropped the ball she'd just caught and scanned back and forth, trying to find the flying object. Suddenly, she ran forward with her gloved hand extended and caught the falling ball.

Joe ran for her when she went off the end of the stage. He caught her in his arms.

She pulled off her blindfold and held the baseball aloft.

Every person was up, cheering, whistling, and applauding. Even Victor and Tracy were up, but not the old man; however, he and his chauffer did applaud her performance.

Joe continued to hold Catalina as she wrapped her arm around his neck and kissed his cheek.

"You did it, Hotshot," Joe said. "You did it!"

"I didn't know you were going to throw it straight up."

"Ha. But I knew you could catch it."

He let go of her, and she stepped back on stage.

"Good job, Pissant." McGill came forward and held out his hand to her. "I think you'll be getting a call from the Mets next season."

She laughed when she took his hand. "Yeah. I could so play first base." She pulled him up onto the stage beside her and whispered near his ear, "And that's 'Ms. Pissant' to you."

"Let me see that." He opened her right palm to examine the array of sensors. "So cool." He gave her one of his rare smiles. "When do I get mine?"

"Do you understand Lidar?"

"No, but I think I'm about to learn."

She removed the sensor pad from her hand and held it out to him.

He turned it over. "Wow, pins."

"Yeah. Two hundred and fifty-six. Watch them closely." She clicked on a switch at the side of her cap.

"They're moving."

"Uh-huh." She swiveled her head from side to side.

"Different patterns."

"Right. Now, place it against your palm."

He did as she said.

"Feel it?"

"Yes," McGill said. "It's like they're tapping out a message."

"Exactly."

"What's it telling me?"

"The Lidar beams from the array on my cap," she touched the three-by-six inch panel above the bill of her hat, "send and receive the laser beams, sorta like sonar. Then the processor converts those signals to a picture of what's out in front of you. That information is then sent to the pin pad and expressed against your palm to tell you what's there."

"I feel the pins tapping in patterns, but how can anyone understand it?"

"You know the story of Helen Keller?"

"Yes, she was deaf, blind, and unable to speak."

"But she learned to speak," Catalina said. "Anne Sullivan taught her by pressing her fingers into Helen's palm, in particular patterns."

"It must have taken a long time."

"Yes, but Helen was very intelligent, like you. She eventually earned a BA degree from Radcliffe."

"Wow."

"I know. Have you ever tried to learn another language?"

"Yes, French," he said.

"When you first started French, what did it sound like to you?"

"Like some kind of gibberish."

"But you eventually learned to speak French, right?"

"Is this French I'm feeling in my hand?"

"No, it's an artificial language, closer to Chinese than anything else."

"What's it called?"

"Catalinia."

"Cool. When are you going to teach me?" he asked.

"Tonight. After you take me to dinner."

He grinned.

"All right, you two, cut it out before I have to hose you down."

"Wow, Tracy," McGill said. "That's the second time in my life I've seen you smile."

"Yes, idiot children always amuse me. Come on, Saylor, someone wants to shake your hand."

"Who?" She followed Tracy toward Victor and the old guy.

"Catalina Saylor," Victor said, "meet Oliver Wendell Qubit."

Without standing, the old man extended a bony hand.

"Oh, my God." Catalina took his hand. "There really is a Mr. Qubit."

"Yes, and I was very impressed with your little exhibition. Victor said I would be amazed, and I must say, I wasn't disappointed."

"Thank you, Mr. Qubit. I could never have done it without your generous assistance."

He let go of her hand. "You might go places," he grinned, "if you could stay out of the lockup."

She laughed. "You know what would be nice, Mr. Qubit?"

"What's that?"

"Sayloooor," Victor said and gave her the eye.

"You know that vacant area, back behind the kitchenette and store room?"

Mr. Qubit glanced that way. "No, but I'll take your word for it."

"It would be a great place for a few pieces of gym equipment."

"You never know when you're ahead," Victor said, "do you, Saylor?"

"I'm just asking."

Mr. Qubit laughed. "It sounds like a grand idea. Good way to keep these people from getting fat and lazy. See to it, Victor." He reached a hand toward his chauffer. "Help me, George. You'll have to excuse me, folks. It's almost nap time for this old man.”

“Thank you, Mr. Qubit,” Catalina said as George supported him and they walked toward the door.

He waved his cane in the air. “Get back to work, Saylor. You’re burning daylight.”

* * * * *

Tracy assigned Catalina to cubicle number forty-one, but she moved into a vacant one next to McGill.

Soon, the sound of an electric hand tool came from her side of the partition.

“What the hell are you doing?” McGill stood to peek over the top.

“I borrowed Joe’s electric screwdriver.”

“I know. All that racket woke me from a nice dream about you taking me to Daniel’s tonight for an elegant dinner.”

“You really were dreaming. My dream was of you escorting me to the Flatiron Room. I’m taking this wall down.”

“Why?”

“Because it’s a great place to get drunk while having a nice meal.”

“No, I mean the wall.”

The last screw dropped to the floor as the wall tilted over toward McGill. He shot out both hands to catch it.

Catalina grinned as he lowered the wall to the floor. “Now I can see you and we don’t have to shout at each other.”

“And it means I have to look at your ugly mug all day.”

“Yeah, you better smile when you say that.” She

126

tossed the screwdriver to him.

* * * * *

After dinner at the Flatiron, they went to his place on the Upper East Side.

"Drink?" McGill stood at the bar separating his kitchen from the dining room.

"No," Catalina said from the other side of the bar.

"Dessert?" He went to the fridge.

"No."

When he turned, she was standing next to him.

"What, then? TV?"

"Shut up." She brushed her lips across his.

"Mmm..." He slipped his hands around her waist. "I think I know what you want."

"Uh-huh."

"Popcorn."

She muzzled him with her lips.

* * * * *

Catalina woke to McGill talking to someone on his bedside phone.

"I want you to meet someone," he said into the phone.

She rolled toward him, lifting her leg across his thighs.

"She's really nice."

He listened for a moment, then looked at Catalina's smile. "Well, she has an adorable wart on the end of her nose with three black hairs–"

She grabbed a handful of his hair.

"Ow!" He turned his naked body toward her. "No,

127

she's not another blonde. In fact, she's bald, but after the chemo–ow!"

"One more time, Mister," Catalina mouthed the words, "and you're going to be missing one of your prized jewels." She ran her hand down across his abdomen, raking her nails on his skin.

"Gotta go, Mom. We'll see you at seven."

* * * * *

"Who is this, Mrs. McGillicuddy?"

Catalina was by the mantel in McGill's parents' home in Bridgeport, Connecticut, where a small brownish picture stood near an elegant BioUrn. Growing from the urn was a perfect little bonsai tree.

"It looks like a tintype," Catalina said.

Mrs. McGillicuddy came from the kitchen, carrying a tray with tea and German chocolate cake. "It's actually a daguerreotype." She set the tray on the coffee table. "They're my great-great-grandparents. That picture was made in eighteen sixty-one, and Mildred, my great-great-grandmother, wrote in her diary that her husband paid the outrageous sum of six dollars for it, which would be about a hundred and ninety dollars in today's money. Would you like milk in your teacup before or after the tea?"

"Before." Catalina touched a fingertip to the picture. *What a beautiful oval frame.*

The End

If you enjoyed reading Raji, Book One, please leave a brief
review on Amazon by clicking the
link below.

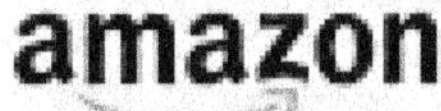

Thank you.

Like me on Facebook → Facebook/charleybrindley

charleybrindley@yahoo.com

www.charleybrindley.com

Charley Brindley is a retired coder living in the Ozarks of
southwest Missouri. He draws on his experiences in the U.
S. Air Force and extensive world travels to write adventure
novels.

Audiobook – Unabridged – Read by Liz Krane
9 hours and 4 minutes

Also available in eBook and paperback format

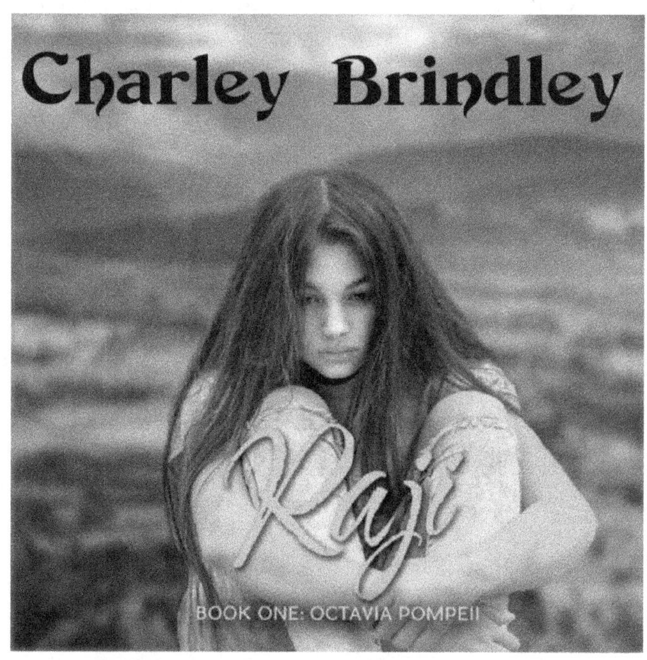

1.

Raji Book One: Octavia Pompeii

December 1925. Vincent Fusilier finds Raji sleeping in his parents' barn. He thinks she's a vagrant and tells her she has to go. She doesn't understand English and doesn't know where she is. Over the next few months, these two teens struggle to understand each other's language and culture.

2.

Raji Book Two: The Academy

August 1926. Raji is accepted into the prestigious Octavia Pompeii Academy. She and Elizabeth Keesler are the only girls in the student body of one hundred cadets and must endure the derision and taunts from ninety-eight boys who would like nothing better than to see them drop out of school. In addition to the contempt of the male students and high academic standards set by the instructors, Raji and Elizabeth must also conform to the strict disciplinary code enforced by the indomitable Elvira Gulch, Director of Development.

3.

Raji Book Three: Dire Kawa

October 1932. At the beginning of the Great Depression, schools and universities all over America were cutting back and even closing their campuses. Raji and Fuse, like so many other young people, were to be cut adrift. Having concentrated on nothing but academics for the past four years, they were not prepared for the brutal economic realities of a world sinking into misery and hopelessness.

4.

Raji Book Four: The House of the West Wind

Fuse returns to Burma in 1941 to look for Kayin. He left Raji behind in Virginia to recuperate from her ordeal, but she promised to join him later in Mandalay. It has been eight years since Fuse and Raji left Burma on the ill-fated training mission to Ethiopia. Since then, he has not heard anything from Kayin. She is probably married by now, or at least in a relationship with someone, but he has to find out, just to be sure she's all right. What he discovers at the old hotel is something completely unexpected.

Oxana's Pit

Oxana uses forced labor to operate an illegal amber mine in the Amazon. Her open-pit excavation is on land owned by Tosh Scarborough. When he discovers Oxana's pit on a satellite photo, he goes to investigate and is captured by Oxana's thugs. One of Tosh's employees, Amber Bravant, organizes a search for him. Oxana is quick to punish and even murder her slave laborers, but what will happen if she gets her hands on Amber?

6.

Ariion XXIII

Ariion Sanders, a disabled teenage girl, is inspired by a homeless man she meets in a New York City jail. The man, Cameron Littleheart St. Lawrence, has been arrested for bank robbery, but without convincing evidence, the judge is forced to release him. The bumbling bank robbers have their loot stolen from them, and they think Cameron took it. After they kidnap Cameron, Ariion hatches a plan for his rescue; however, her scheme goes awry, and she finds herself in deep trouble.

7.

Cian

Cian and Saxon's meeting in the heart of the Amazon is more than an encounter of two people; it's the coming together of two different worlds. Their explorations and adventures take them deep into the rain forest, then halfway around the globe in search of a peaceful place to settle down. But instead of finding peace, their shared sense of justice finds them traveling from Europe to New York, then back to Brazil, where they must confront the evil network of the ambitious and heartless Oxana, who will stop at nothing to advance her trade in endangered animals, as well as women and little girls.

8.

The Last Seat on the Hindenburg

A misdialed phone number brings Donovan to Sandia's front door. He thought he was to teach Braille to a blind person, while she thought he was a disability attorney. When Donovan learns of Sandia's and her grandfather's dreadful circumstances, the Braille lesson is forgotten and he embarks on a mission to help Sandia solve the several dilemmas that threaten to overwhelm her.

9.

The Sea of Tranquility 2.0: Book One

An exasperated high school social science teacher with half her senior class failing, resorts to a drastic measure, resulting in The Sea of Tranquility 2.0. Four of her students come up with a radical project to help slow rising sea levels and provide a homeland for some of the millions of refugees set adrift by wars, failing economies, and gang violence.

10.

The Sea of Tranquility 2.0: Book Two

Monica, Harry, and Caitlion try to find a way to communicate with the Jamori nomads they left behind in the Safandel Desert. While working hard to finish their senior year of high school, they're also working on details of their plan to gain funding for the Sea of Tranquility 2.0 project.

11.

The Sea of Tranquility 2.0 Book Three: The Sand Vipers

When Sikandar's homeland is invaded, he must return to defend his people. Monica defies him, refusing to stay behind, insisting she will not lose him again. The two of them, plus the Gang of Four, set off for the remote and desolate outback of Alcina Sahar, where Sikandar is certain his people have taken refuge.

12.

The Sea of Tranquility 2.0 Book Four: The Republic
Monica and Sikandar, along with the Gang of Eight, open the first pipeline to siphon seawater to the Sea of Tranquility 2.0. Will it work? Scientists are divided on the theory of a nine-foot wide pipe reaching 156 miles across the desert that will actually pull water from the ocean unassisted by any pumps. If it works, the new City of Tranquility will flourish; if not, the desert will reclaim what little work has been done.

13.

Dragonfly vs Monarch: Book One

Autumn Willow is a grad student at MIT. In her spare time, she co-pilots her grandfather's B-17, a restored WWII bomber. Sasha Brezhnev is a pilot for the Russian Air Force, flying the SU-57 fighter jet. She is assigned seek-and-destroy missions over the Safandel Desert in central Anddor Shallau, where terrorists are covertly working to destroy the country's democratic government. Rigger Entime is an engineer working on a CIA project to develop a tiny drone aircraft to be used in surveillance and possibly carry out assassinations of terrorists' leaders.

14.

Dragonfly vs Monarch: Book Two

The Dragonfly and Monarch are tiny drone aircraft designed to resemble actual insects. They can flitter around military installations and terrorists' camps without being noticed while they collect video data about these installations and the people in charge. On their first mission over an isolated stretch of desert, their remote pilots, one American and one Russian, are drawn into a strange struggle to survive. In their attempt to retrieve their disabled drones, the pilots discover a shocking secret about themselves.

15.

Hannibal's Elephant Girl

In 218 BCE, Hannibal took his army, along with 27 elephants, over the Alps to attack the Romans. Eleven years before this historic event, on the banks of a river near Carthage, in North Africa, one of his elephants pulled a drowning girl from the turbulent waters. Thus began Liada's epic journey with the elephant known as Obolus.

16.

Hannibal's Elephant Girl, Book Two
The Voyage to Iberia

Liada and the slave girl, Tin Tin Ban Sunia, sail away from Carthage with Hannibal, on their way to Iberia. Also on board is Obolus, Hannibal's prized war elephant. Not only do they have to deal with pirates and Roman galleys, Sulobo the slave master and Sukal the javelineer are on the ship, too, just waiting for a chance to wreak vengeance on the two girls.

17.

Sea of Sorrows Book 2 of The Rod of God
An old man returns to Thailand after a fifty-year absence. When he was in Bangkok on leave from the Vietnam War, he met a girl and fell in love. After returning to the battlefield, he was critically wounded and shipped to a hospital in San Diego. After recovering from his injuries he goes back to Bangkok looking for Chayan, but she's not there. A year later he returns and one of the other girls tells him Chayan died during a typhoid epidemic. Devastated, he returns to the States, goes to medical school and eventually starts a family. Now, after fifty years, he goes again to Bangkok, but instead of Chayan, he finds his past had been evolving without him.

18.

The Last Mission of the Seventh Cavalry

A unit of the Seventh Cavalry is on a mission over Afghanistan when their plane is hit by something. The soldiers bail out of the crippled plane, but when the thirteen men and women reach the ground, they are not in Afghanistan. Not only are they four thousand miles from their original destination but it appears they have descended two thousand years into the past where primitive forces fight each other with swords and arrows. The platoon is thrown into a battle where they must choose sides quickly or die. They are swept along in a tide of events so powerful that their courage, ingenuity and weapons are tested to the limits of their durability and strength.

19.

Do Not Resuscitate

A dying man tells his great granddaughter that he has signed a Do Not Resuscitate document, giving instructions for medical personal to let him die if he's determined to be brain dead. He's invited on a long journey that he thinks is taking place in his subconscious mind as his body is being kept alive against his wishes. What unfolds before him may be an elaborate hallucination caused by the psychedelic effect of the anticholinergic drugs being pumped through his body, or are these strange and cathartic events actually happening?

20.

The Rod of God, Book One: The Edge of Disaster

Staff Sergeant Saxon "Pagan" McKenzie and Tech Sergeant William "Choir Boy" Kabilis are involved in a nuclear accident during the Cuban Missile Crisis. Not only does it threaten to set off World War III, but it sends McKenzie and Kabilis on a journey into the first days of the Vietnam War.

149

21.

Henry IX

The queen of England is 93 years old. The process of installing a new monarch is already being organized.

Her son, Prince Charles, is the heir apparent. However, someone is attempting to alter the line of succession.

There are over 140 people in line to become monarch. If Prince Charles is for any reason, unable to ascend, then the next in line, Prince William, will become King. If he is unavailable, Prince George will be next in line, and so on, down the list.

Evil plans are being executed.

Lady Pion Ciana Victoria Lancaster, known to her friends as 'Ciana', is number thirty-seven. William

George Tindall Mountbatten is number thirty-eight on the list of Royals.

Wearing a disguise and going by the name of 'Scipio' William Mountbatten accidentally meets Ciana in a London pub.

Long ago, a general famously said, 'All battle plans fall apart upon first contact with the enemy.' That is exactly what happened when Ciana and Scipio come together.

22. 

Casper's Game

Bell Casper is running a stealthy game in the Blue Parrot, a swanky bar in Manhattan catering to wealthy pleasure seekers. The game seems shady, and maybe it is. Leticia pretends to be his assistant.

She's twenty-four and Bell's twenty-seven. Their relationship isn't clear. Gigi is a pretty blonde, twenty-five years old. She also works out of the bar, running her own racket. She's attracted to Bell, but she can't understand why Bell and Leticia are together, or what his game is all about. She's determined to unravel both mysteries.

Coming Soon

23. *Dragonfly vs Monarch, Book Three*

Theodore Breckinridge (Pug) and Rio Lujan join forces to rescue Autumn and **Sasha**.

24. *Hannibal's Elephant Girl: Book Three*

Liada and her friend, Tin Tin Ban Sunia, struggle to fit into their new environment in Iberia.

25. *Still Waters Run Deep*

A precious five-year-old girl is accidentally imbedded with five gigabytes of medical information.

26. *Ms Machiavelli*

The teenage daughter of the famous Italian, Nioccolo Machiavelli, makes her mark during the Renaissance.

27. *The Last Mission of the Seventh Cavalry, Book Two*

The soldiers of the Seventh must mount a rescue mission for the stranded astronauts after they came down from the International Space Station in the escape pod.

28. *Ariion XXIX*

In the year 2219 Ariion XXIX is her third rotation as quadrant perimeter analog. She has jurisdiction along the outer beacons of our solar sphere, encompassing all ten planets and their moons, both natural and artificial. She is the 29th Ariion in a long line Ariions stretching back to the first Ariion, born in Valdacia in the year 221 BCE.

29. *The Journey to Valdacia*

A satellite cartographer has discovered on his latest photos, the ruins of an ancient city in the Sahara Desert. It has been uncovered by a recent sandstorm and Donny slips away from his job at xxx to go explore the ruins before anyone else, especially his colleague, Kelli, spots the location of what appears to be a very large city. Before he can reach the ruins, he's entangled in secret and deadly activity.